W9-CXU-456

周
春
珠

Spring Pearl The LAST FLOWER

GIRLS *of* MANY LANDS

England ⇒ 1592
Isabel: Taking Wing by Annie Dalton

France ⇒ 1711
Cécile: Gates of Gold by Mary Casanova

China ⇒ 1857
Spring Pearl: The Last Flower by Laurence Yep

Yup'ik Alaska ⇒ 1890
Minuk: Ashes in the Pathway by Kirkpatrick Hill

India ⇒ 1939
Neela: Victory Song by Chitra Banerjee Divakaruni

Spring Pearl
The LAST FLOWER

by Laurence Yep

American Girl

Published by Pleasant Company Publications
Copyright © 2002 by Pleasant Company

Visit our Web site at **americangirl.com**

Printed in China.
02 03 04 05 06 07 C&C 10 9 8 7 6 5 4 3 2 1

Girls of Many Lands™, Spring Pearl™, and American Girl®
are trademarks of Pleasant Company.

PERMISSIONS & PICTURE CREDITS
The following individuals and organizations have generously given
permission to reprint illustrations contained in "Then and Now":
p. 199—© Historical Picture Archive/CORBIS (Canton house);
pp. 200–201—The Minneapolis Institute of Arts (tunic and silk pouch);
pp. 202–203—Photograph courtesy Peabody Essex Museum, Salem, MA,
neg. A9392 (women with bound feet); © Carl & Ann Purcell/CORBIS
(food market); pp. 204–205—Hulton Archive/Getty Images (Canton
houseboats); Forrest Anderson/TimePix (Chinese schoolgirls).

Illustration by Kazuhiko Sano

Library of Congress Cataloging-in-Publication Data

Yep, Laurence.
Spring Pearl : the last flower / by Laurence Yep.

p. cm — (Girls of many lands)

Summary: Called boyish by her new family for being able to read and write,
twelve-year-old orphaned Spring Pearl's "odd ways" help save the family
during the 1857 Opium War in Canton, China.

ISBN 1-58485-519-3 (pbk.) — ISBN 1-58485-595-9

1. Guangzhou (China)—History—19th century—Juvenile fiction.
2. China—History—Foreign intervention, 1857–1861—Juvenile fiction.
[1. Guangzhou (China)—History—19th century—Juvenile fiction.
2. China—History—Foreign intervention, 1857–1861—Fiction.
3. Family life—China—Guangzhou—Fiction.
4. Orphans—Fiction. 5. Sex role—Fiction.] I. Title. II. Series.
PZ7.Y44 Sp 2002 [Fic]—dc21 2001008750

To Felicia, Cory, and Lee,
and all their many "cousins"
in this brave new world

Contents

1 *The Lost Garden*

"Miss," the boy said, "we should be going."

"Just one more moment, please," I said. He probably couldn't understand why anyone would want to stay longer.

In that instant, I saw my home through his eyes. I had let things become shabby while Mother had been sick. The paper on the windows had become tattered and the bamboo walls were badly in need of repair. There was dust everywhere. The few sticks of furniture were pieces no one had wanted to buy. The table and chairs were old and battered, with wobbly legs. Yet in my mind's eye, I could see Mother sitting in one while she sewed. I could see Father in another, staring off into space before he began painting furiously. And I was there with them, balanced on a stool, trying not to fall off it while I did my lessons.

In the corner lay the straw mat, and I looked away quickly. Mother had breathed her last there. The landlord had been quite upset when he found out she had died inside. He would have to reduce the rent to attract new tenants who might think my mother's ghost was haunting our cottage. Even if that were true, her gentle soul would never harm anyone.

I ran my hands over my jacket. It had been one of the last things Mother had made. The silk had been a gift from Father's friend, Master Sung. I smoothed it over my sides, feeling the cool lightness. Mother had sewn camellias, which were her favorite flowers, on the hems and cuffs. They looked so real, I could almost smell the scent. When I touched my jacket, I felt her love surround me, keeping me safe from harm.

"Please, Miss, I have other chores," the boy begged. He looked several years older than me, with a pleasant round face and small eyes.

"Yes, of course." I started to reach for my basket.

The boy smiled. "I'll take that, Miss. It'd be worth my hide if anyone saw you doing my work."

I pulled my hand back. "Your arms are already full."

"All I need is that bamboo pole outside," the boy said and suddenly grinned. He had my measure by now. "You never had servants, Miss?"

I shook my head. "We did everything ourselves." Guiltily, I thought that if Mother had had more help than just me, she might still be alive.

Setting down the other basket, he disappeared through the doorway and came back a moment later with a pole two meters long. "I think I saw some rope lying around."

"Yes, it's right here." Wanting to be helpful, I bent over for the coil of old cord by my foot and started to pick it up.

The boy held up his hand. "Wait, Miss."

I paused in mid-bend. "That's silly. It's right here."

"You're well spoken, Miss—in fact, better than the ladies of our household," the boy said. "And your manners are certainly better. But if I may be so bold, I have to tell you there's more to being a lady than speech and polite ways. A lady should never do her own lifting."

"But—" I began.

He snatched up the cord before I could get it. "As my granny says, 'Does a bird tell a fish how to swim?' Master Sung's household will be a lot different than your old home here."

"But I'm not helpless," I said, annoyed.

He dipped his head respectfully. "I can see that, Miss. But if you act like a servant, then the Sungs'll treat you like one."

Proudly, I repeated what I had told Master Sung. "I intend to earn my keep."

The boy laughed, just as Master Sung had. "Oh, the Sungs'll see that you do." He paused and added, "I know it's not my place to say, but you're moving in with the sharks."

It was my turn to laugh. "Master Sung is no shark! And he has told me about his children; they sounded quite human to me."

He nodded to the basket I had been filling with books. "I can see you're a learned person. You must have read how looks aren't everything. The sweetest little old auntie could be a tiger in disguise."

I folded my arms. "I've read the folktales."

The boy was quick to pick up on my doubts. "As my granny says, 'Every tree starts out as a seed.' And it doesn't matter how much make-believe there is now, it had to begin with a bit of truth."

"Well, I'll be careful," I said, trying not to smile in amusement. "Thank you for the warning."

"I may not be able to read or write, but I'm a regular professor when it comes to surviving the Sungs." The boy measured out the cord quickly against his forearm and then set it at a selected spot in his teeth. The cord, though old, was thick.

"I think I have some scissors in one of my baskets," I offered.

To my amazement, the boy bit the cord clean through. Clicking his teeth, he grinned. "You've never had my granny's dumplings. My kin have two types of teeth: strong or gone."

With the efficiency that came of practice, the boy tied a basket to either end of the pole. "And what is your name?" I asked.

"I answer to 'Doggy,' Miss," the boy said. Squatting,

he set the pole over his shoulder. When he straightened, the pole bowed in the middle but did not break.

"My name is Chou Spring Pearl," I said.

He dipped his head respectfully toward the doorway. "Miss Pearl. If you please?"

As I crossed the threshold, sadness squeezed my insides so much that I almost gasped.

"Don't look back, Miss," Doggy whispered. "Never look back."

I took a ragged breath. "Yes, you're right."

However, it hurt almost as much to step outside into our little garden. Mother had been so proud of it. The three of us had spent many sunny afternoons painting and studying and sewing there. After a rain, it had always smelled so fresh. The plants and flowers there had given me so many happy memories that they were like cousins.

I looked over at the spot where Father had died a year ago. Some white jasmine was still blooming on the bamboo fence. When Mother had been able to tend it, it had been a wall of white, and we had used the flowers in tea. Now old vines choked the new growth like tangles of cord, and leaves littered the ground beneath.

There weren't even any birds to bid me farewell—during the many recent rebellions and wars, the city's poor folk had trapped and eaten all of them. Weeds had taken over, and only a few flowers, like the fragrant plumeria, still battled for space and life.

I began to feel an ache inside, as if I were mourning my parents again. Perhaps I couldn't save all of the flowers here, but I was determined to save something.

Anxiously, I waded through the knee-high weeds, hunting for the camellias. My parents had loved them, painting and sewing them up to the last. Father had long ago written a poem on one of his paintings of camellias, calling them a pearl given by nature. Mother had liked both the painting and poem so much that she had named me "Spring Pearl."

"Miss?" Doggy called impatiently. "What are you doing?"

"Wait," I said, hunting desperately. Finally I found one survivor almost buried under the invaders.

While Doggy stood impatiently, I dug it up carefully

and put it in an old pot.

"Why would you want that old thing?" he asked.

"Just because . . . I want it," I said, not wishing to reveal the real meaning to a stranger.

With a sigh, he found a space in the basket and put the flower inside. As he shuffled forward, I squared my shoulders. Doggy was right. Don't look back. My old home was already gone. I had to keep telling myself that as I strode to the gate. The closer I got, though, the more my stomach tightened with fear.

What would become of me now that my parents were dead?

Even as Mother lay dying, she had wept with worry for me. I had told her over and over that I would be all right. Now it was time to keep my word. Taking a deep breath, I plunged outside, away from my old life and into the new.

2 *The Rats' Nest*

As Doggy and I started on our way, the autumn air was so still that I could smell the stink of the Pearl River that ran through the heart of Canton. Sometimes the collected odors from the river had overpowered even my mother's flowers. The rest of Canton sneered at our neighborhood, calling it the "Rats' Nest." Since the river smelled so bad sometimes, most people preferred to live away from its banks. But in the last few centuries, poor folk had taken over the open spaces. Even though they didn't own the land, they had thrown together shacks out of sticks, and no one had stopped them. Other huts were made of mud that barely held up through the monsoon rains. Our little bamboo house was one of the few places that was actually legal. And it was a palace compared to our neighbors' homes.

"She's here!" Auntie Wong shouted as Doggy and I turned a corner and stepped into her small stall. Then she thrust a small bundle into my hand. "Take this, child." It was the eve of the Moon Festival, and I could smell the moon cakes the bundle held. Auntie Wong's were the best, and she traveled about the city selling her buns and pastries. She wasn't my real aunt, but she acted like one. "Only twelve and an orphan." She shook her head. "What's to become of you?"

"Thank you, Auntie," I said, using my free arm to hug her. "Mother and I would have starved without your help."

She gave me a little squeeze and then pushed me away. "Your father wrote all those letters and petitions for me and never took a penny."

"Father was happy to help you with that lawsuit," I told her. "That man should have paid up right away."

Auntie's call had brought other people out from their shacks and stalls, and now she was acting as a sentry to keep back the small crowd that had gathered.

"Knowing Auntie Wong, she was probably overcharging," Uncle Soo laughed. His robe had spots of blood from his work as a butcher. He held out a cylindrical-shaped package. "Here."

As I took the cylinder, I recognized the material. It was the backing that Father had used at one time for his paintings. "But this is yours. Father gave it to you."

"And I got my payment from looking at it all these years," Uncle Soo said. "So now I'm passing it on."

"But we can't give the beef back," I said, trying to return the package.

Uncle Soo became unusually serious. "I know you had to sell everything for your mother's medicines. You ought to have one of your father's paintings."

"Take it," Auntie Wong urged. "If anyone over-charged anyone, it's this old bandit of a butcher."

I knew my parents would not have wanted me to take the painting back. As they liked to say, "We might not have money, but we're not beggars." But the painting seemed glued to my hand.

Close to tears, I could only nod my head gratefully.

"Oh, here, child. We don't want those rich folk to think we Rats don't have style, too," Auntie's son

Hammer said, and he added a European spittoon
to the load in my arms. "It's something I . . . um . . .
found." Hammer was a big, strapping young man
who loaded and unloaded ships and who was always
"finding" useful things.

Auntie Wong slapped Hammer on the arm. "Now
what's Pearl going to do with a thing like that?"

"A young lady can always use a nice vase," Hammer
said indignantly.

Auntie Wong dinged a finger against the brass side.
"Foreigners spit into this, you idiot."

"You're the idiot," Hammer argued stubbornly.
"You don't want Pearl spitting on the rich man's floor,
do you?"

My father used to say that receiving a gift was more
of an art than giving one. "Thank you. I'll treasure it
always," I assured him.

"See?" Hammer said triumphantly. "Only a high-
class lady would have her own personal spittoon. You
just say the word. I know where I can find some polish
for you, too."

Nearly everyone on the street turned out with a gift.

Many were small items, but they were all that my fellow Rats could afford. Even the gamblers interrupted their game long enough to hand me several dice.

"For luck," they said with knowing winks. The cubes felt heavier on one side, so I knew they were weighted for cheating.

"You'll always have a place here in the Rats' Nest," Auntie Wong promised.

Somehow Doggy either stowed the gifts away in the baskets or tied them to the pole. He had quite a load by the time we left the Rats' Nest. Even so, he handled it easily.

I hadn't been able to afford a proper funeral for Mother; and since there hadn't been a public wake, I hadn't known so many people cared about her or Father. "I wish my parents could have seen how much they were loved," I said, brushing my eyes with my fingers.

"It wasn't just them that was loved," Doggy observed.

"But I didn't do anything," I said. "I can't paint like Father, and I'm hopeless with a needle." I thought of the kilometers of thread I'd wasted and the blood I had bled from my fingertips while I had tried to learn to sew from my mother.

"But you must have other talents," Doggy said.

"I have a fair hand," I said, and then shook my head, "but no talent for words. I usually have to copy the form letters in the book whenever someone wants to send mail." Father had a book of form letters that could be copied, with the person's name added. That wouldn't have been good enough for Father's scholarly friends, but it was just fine for my fellow Rats in our Nest.

"And do you charge them?" Doggy asked.

"I wouldn't think of it," I said, horrified.

"There you go," he said. "And I'm sure you've done other things."

"Well," I admitted, "I did help Uncle Soo with his accounts. He can slice beef thin as paper, but he's hopeless when it comes to addition."

Doggy chuckled. "Well, Miss, and how many other hopeless cases live in the Rats' Nest?"

"I never counted them before," I said, adding them up in my mind. "But I guess there were quite a few."

"I bet they kept you busy," he said.

To me, it was so simple. "They needed help."

"There are some folks who always walk away from any mess," Doggy observed, "and there's some folks who always tidy up."

In my mind, I went through the crowd and realized I'd actually helped each of them. So perhaps Doggy was right. My fellow Rats would miss *me* as well as my parents. Instead of making me feel better, however, realizing it only made me feel worse to be leaving my friends behind.

We continued walking along the river and soon passed the remains of the foreigners' warehouses and offices, an area known as the "Thirteen Factories." Nothing had actually been made there, but the foreign merchants who bought and sold things for other people had called themselves "factors," an old British word for "agents."

The buildings had been looted and torched months ago, after the foreigners left Canton because of the

war, but the smell of smoke clung to the ruins. Here
and there a burnt post still rose like a giant stick of
charcoal above the piles of sooty bricks.

Father used to like to sketch the little garden
next to the factories, and I used to tag along for the
wonderful spectacle. The Chinese government had
not allowed the foreigners to leave that area, but
curious Chinese had been drawn there to watch the
foreigners' strange antics. Mealtimes drew the biggest
crowds, as people jostled to peek through the windows
at the foreigners who put sugar in their tea! And
instead of cutting up their meat in the kitchen like
sensible folk, the foreigners insisted on hacking away
like butchers at big slabs of it on the dining table itself.

And where there was a ready audience, jugglers and
acrobats and storytellers had also gone. Then came
peddlers to sell food and souvenirs to the crowd. The
Thirteen Factories had become the best show in the
city, and all for free. But that was all gone now. Once
the war between China and Britain had started again
almost a year ago, the foreigners had been forced out
and their businesses destroyed.

As I stared at what had once been Mr. Fortescue's establishment, I hoped our good friend had escaped. If there had been more foreigners like Mr. Fortescue, the opium trade would have ended. He hated the drug that destroyed so many lives.

Mr. Fortescue was a British merchant who had admired Father's garden sketch and tried to strike up a conversation. Their very first attempts had been through signs, but their communication improved as Mr. Fortescue learned some Chinese and Father—and I—learned a little English. Mr. Fortescue eventually commissioned my father to paint landscapes of the city so that he could see what Canton looked like.

Over the years, they had become fast friends. And through Mr. Fortescue, we had made other foreign friends.

Everything had been going along fine until last year, which in the foreign calendar was 1856, when an imperial Chinese official had seized some Chinese criminals who were serving on the crew of a British ship called the *Arrow*. I think in normal times we could have worked it out with them. However, the

British had been looking for an excuse to fight, and so they had declared war. Fifteen years earlier, the British had gone to war to force us to allow them to sell their drugs in China. When they won that war, they had demanded all sorts of trading rights, as well as land for their own city, Hong Kong, which lay to the south-east. Now, it seemed, the British wanted even more from us, and they were again willing to use force.

Another foreign people called the French had joined in, too. There were rumors that the French had their eye on seizing an area called Viet Nam from China's control.

Because of all these troubles in the southeastern provinces of the empire, China's emperor had placed a tough-minded official called Viceroy Yeh over the governors, including the province's governor, Po. This viceroy had refused the foreigners' demands and instead had placed a bounty on the head of every foreign soldier or sailor. The foreign ships retaliated by coming up the Pearl River, blasting a hole through the outer city wall, and sending troops to capture the viceroy himself. But though the viceroy was said to be enormously fat, he had been nimble enough to escape the foreign kidnappers. And although the foreigners had taken the city, they had too few men to hold a half-million people captive for long.

The foreign ships finally retreated after the viceroy attacked them with floating torpedoes recently devised by a clever American mechanic. All of Canton had celebrated the viceroy's great victory.

Doggy and I now turned our backs on the river and walked north. We entered the area known as the Western Suburbs, where many merchants and crafts-people lived and worked. Signs hung in front of the shops. You could tell what was sold in each shop from the shape of the sign. One street was all candle makers. Another had incense sticks—though the pungent air could have told you that. A third street sold glue. Gold and silk and every sort of raw stuff came from all over China and the South Seas to these little shops. From them flowed jewelry, fans, and objects for which the rest of the world clamored.

I paused at the corner where Father had always set up his small table and chair. His paper signs still were pasted to the wall: "Letters and Portraits by a Student of the Academy of Hangchou."

I always helped him set up his little stand and mixed his ink for him. If I closed my eyes, I could almost see him there, sitting proudly on his chair, waiting for a customer.

"Do you want me to go first, Miss?" Doggy asked. "I'll clear the way."

I drew my eyebrows together, puzzled. "I can trade elbows with the best of them." I demonstrated with quick jabs of my elbows what I had learned from years of shopping crowded market stalls.

He pressed his lips together as if holding something back.

"What did I do wrong now?" I asked.

"I wouldn't show that technique to the Sungs, Miss," he said. The laughter finally broke from him.

"Well, they *must* go shopping," I said.

"Yes, but a servant is like the prow of a ship," Doggy explained. "He or she breaks the waves."

"But you've got my baskets," I protested. "Really. Don't worry about me. I can take care of myself."

Doggy sighed. "I don't doubt that, Miss, but that's not the point. If all the rich folk took care of themselves, us servants'd be out of a job. You may think you're being nice by saving us some trouble, but you'll just make some servants snicker."

"For not being a bother?" I asked, puzzled.

Doggy looked silently to Heaven, as if for divine strength, and then lowered his eyes back to me. "I'm not saying it's right, but here's the way of things: Some servants can be more stuck-up than their masters and mistresses. Sort of the reflected glory, you see. So if you act like a servant, they'll treat you like one."

I rubbed my temple. "It doesn't make sense."

"Yes, Miss," Doggy said politely. "Now, if I may be so bold . . . ?"

I nodded for him to go ahead of me. Despite the pole and baskets, he wove his way nimbly through the crowd. Behind him, he left a space in which I could walk in peace.

"Scissors sharp, scissors sharp!" one peddler cried, clashing a pair of scissors together in rhythm to the cry. "Shears, daggers, knives—I'll sharpen them all, lady, so you can cut one of your fine hairs." He stopped when he peered at me closely. "Oh, it's you, Spring Pearl. Aren't you done up all fancy today. Going to get married?"

"No," I said. I wasn't sure what to tell him I was going to be doing, since I didn't know myself.

The peanut peddler and the vegetable seller didn't recognize me in my fancy clothes, either, but they backed off once they saw who I was. We grinned at one another because they knew how hard a bargain I could drive.

We crossed a creek whose murky water some poet had named the "Jade Stone Belt" in a fit of fancy. Before us rose the Old City wall that was some eight meters wide and fifteen meters thick. Together with the walls around the southern area called the New City, it ran for over nine and a half kilometers.

In an open space in front of the wall's broad gate, Chinese and Manchu soldiers were practicing with big cutlasses, slicing at invisible foreign invaders. Because there were not enough regular soldiers to guard the long walls, clans from all over the province had sent their warriors to defend Canton from the foreign invasion. Some of these clan warriors were practicing with the soldiers. Except for their special badges and weapons, the clan warriors dressed and wore their hair like normal civilians.

The Manchus, a people from the north, had conquered China two hundred years ago and now ruled the empire. They had taken over part of the Western Suburbs of the Old City. They made all Chinese men wear their hair in queues, like the tails of the horses that the Manchus had ridden to victory.

Perhaps the Manchus' ancestors might have been tough enough to keep out the British and French, but their descendants had grown fat and lazy from living off the Chinese. These Manchu soldiers' uniforms were stained, and we could smell the stink of liquor as we passed them.

The street we were on ran unusually straight for Canton. Over the last two thousand years, the houses and shops had squeezed together, forming a maze of narrow lanes and alleys. Over the rooftops, I saw the top stories of the eight-sided Flowery Pagoda that the poet Su Tung P'o had so admired, and near it rose the minaret of a mosque that served the Chinese Moslems from the western provinces. Rising from a hill in the north were the red-tiled roofs of the Five-Stories Pagoda.

Across the street that ran straight and true to the great North Gate, we entered the Chinese section. Here, monasteries and government buildings rubbed shoulder-to-shoulder with schools and the homes of officials and scholars.

We turned past several arches built to honor famous scholars and entered a small square.

"Hey!" Doggy suddenly shouted. Next to a building were several sedan chairs, which were chairs balanced on poles and carried between two men. Some were covered on the sides and had curtained windows. Others were completely open.

The sedan carriers scrambled to their feet at Doggy's hail. "If you want to get there fast, use us," one man called.

"His feet stink so bad, you'll choke halfway," another said. "Use us. Our chairs are clean, and so are we."

"Really, Doggy," I said, "I can walk."

"Lesson Number Two, Miss," Doggy said. "Never walk when you can ride."

Doggy inspected the chairs. He selected one with little curtains to screen the inside and then bargained with the carriers. They argued and swore, but when they were done, they were all grinning. I think the argument was some kind of game to them. And though both sides pretended outwardly to be unhappy with the deal, inside I think they were satisfied.

"Miss." Doggy drew aside the curtain to let me sit on the cushioned chair. Because the pillow was thick and clean, I had thought, like Doggy, that it was one of the better ones.

However, the fancy cushion hid the fact that some of the bamboo slats of the seat were broken. As the carriers lifted the chair into the air with a grunt, I felt myself sag so alarmingly that I clung to the side. Doggy walked in front of the first carrier, leading the way.

As precarious as the seat was, I still enjoyed the novelty of a ride. The street rose at a gentle incline, and I could not resist peeking out the window. We passed a wealthy monastery where all the statues were freshly painted or gilded. Over the monastery's walls, I saw treetops that probably marked a meditation garden.

On either side, hidden by more long, high walls, were the mansions of the ancient families who had helped rule the empire for centuries. No windows broke the surface, but through some of the open gates, I saw beautiful courtyards and large houses. Though Master Sung was only a merchant, he had bought a scholarly degree that gave him the status of a gentle-man, and I knew he lived in this area.

Finally we came to the highest, longest wall of all. To anyone else, it would have been the sign of a palace.

Why, then, did I feel like I was entering a prison?

3 *The Cage*

Doggy turned sideways, expertly keeping the baskets from swaying too much. With his foot, he kicked at the gate. "Hey, open up. Miss Chou's here."

"Coming, coming," an old man said. His voice creaked almost as much as the gates did when he swung them open. He peered at Doggy through clouded eyes. "She's quite the lass, Doggy."

"She's behind me, Wing," Doggy said, and then grinned over his shoulder at me. "He's quite the joker, old Wing is. He sees better than he lets on, so don't let him play his tricks on you." As he stepped inside, he shook his head. "They should have retired you ten years ago, Wing."

"And miss seeing your execution?" old Wing said. "I'll stick around at least for the trial."

He stepped to the side as Doggy led the way in, but old Wing winked at me as the chair passed.

When the carriers set the chair down, Doggy paid them in cash. "She's really such a little thing, I should only pay you half," he joked to them. As I stepped down from the chair, I noticed both the granite stones that paved the large courtyard and the weeds that grew through the cracks of some of the broken ones.

What impressed me most was the quiet. After the noise and the commotion of the streets, it was strange to come into such a peaceful place. I might as well have been on an island.

Stone columns supported tiled roofs to form a veranda that shaded the other three sides of the courtyard. Carved wooden screens and rice paper covered the windows of the rooms. Large stone jars in front of them must have held flowers once; now they held only weeds, if anything at all.

"Don't gawk, Miss," Doggy whispered as he put the rest of his cash up his sleeve.

Suddenly, I understood his little trick.

"Doggy," I said in a low voice, "were you supposed to

bring the chair to the house to pick me up?"

"You got carried on the part that matters," Doggy chuckled. "Call it your fee to Professor Doggy. But put a frown on your face. Your troubles are starting." He strutted toward a pair of girls lounging on the steps. From the expensive silk of their clothes, I thought they were Master Sung's daughters, but before I could bow, Doggy stopped me. "Not them, Miss. As my granny told me, 'A new hen has to learn who she can peck and who can peck her.'"

Then, lifting his foot, he poked the larger one rudely.

"Hey, Snow Goose, tell the family that Miss Chou is here," he said.

Snow Goose shoved his foot away angrily. "Don't show that filthy thing to me. It's covered in street mud."

He wagged his foot back and forth. "Better than being covered in gutter mud like you. Now do your job."

Snow Goose rose slowly, staring at me insolently, and then sauntered off. Her friend studied me. "So you're the crazy man's daughter."

"He was a famous painter," I said.

"If he was so famous," the girl shrugged, "why are you living on our charity?"

"The last time I asked, this was Master Sung's house and not yours. So he can do what he likes," Doggy corrected her.

I could feel the blood rushing to my cheeks. "It's just temporary," I said, "until I can figure out what to do."

Doggy shot an exasperated look at me even as the girl laughed sullenly. "That's what all leeches say," she sneered.

Then Snow Goose came back. "Master Sung says he'll be free in a bit, but in the meantime you can meet the rest of the family."

Doggy dipped his head. "I'll bring your things to your room, Miss."

"My camellia . . ." I protested.

"I'll keep it safe," Doggy promised and leaned forward to whisper, "Good luck. You're jumping right in with the sharks."

Snow Goose led me across the front courtyard and into a second one, where the family lived. Rooms with verandas lay on three sides, and in the center there was what once had been a garden but what now looked like a scrap of wilderness. It was ten times larger than our little plot back at home, but it was in far worse shape. The weeds were as high as my waist, almost overwhelming everything else. The liquidambar trees on one edge were badly in need of trimming, and their orange leaves littered the walkways.

"What happened to the garden?" I asked, shocked.

"The gardener died two years ago," Snow Goose shrugged. "And they never replaced him."

I glanced around. Although the garden was surrounded on all four sides, it got the full afternoon sun. "It's a shame to let it go to waste."

"The misses are waiting," Snow Goose said pointedly. She was already walking away from me, and I hurried after her, crunching dead leaves under my feet.

As we entered a room in the right wing of the mansion, I heard enough yelling for a rooster fight. The maid didn't take any notice, but went right in.

"Miss Chou," she announced in a shout.

The room fell silent as I entered. The sweet smell of

incense tickled my nose. Three girls lounged in chairs, fanning themselves with expensive fans. The oldest looked about my age.

Each of them was dressed well enough to be a princess. The servants, in their fancy clothes, now seemed almost shabby compared to them.

The oldest girl was wearing a dazzling jacket of many long but narrow chevrons, each a different color. The chevrons looked like angular rainbows, marching one after another. The girl's hair rose above her head in four large loops.

Snapping her ivory-handled fan shut, she said, "I am Miss Emerald." She used the fan to point at the others in turn. "And these are my sisters, Miss Willow and Miss Oriole." I could feel her eyes appraising me as carefully as my mother had inspected a piece of cloth.

"I'm Chou Spring Pearl," I said, giving my full name.

Miss Emerald smiled slyly. "Not Miss Ratty?"

"Pardon?" I asked.

"We heard you came from the Rats' Nest, whatever that is," Miss Oriole piped up. I would have said she was eight and Miss Willow about ten.

Miss Oriole was dressed in a blue jacket and pants with an intricate geometric design of diamonds and squares. Her hair was coiled into a bun on either side of the top of her head and decorated with little gold hairpins in the shapes of animals.

"She lived in a shack in the slum," Miss Willow explained to her sister in a loud voice. She wanted to make sure that I knew she didn't approve of my former home.

Miss Willow wore a jacket and trousers of a tan color with a complicated design of waves in gold thread. Her hair had been twisted into braids that were woven intricately into a bun above the crown of her head, so that her head seemed to tilt forward. Strands of loose hair had been carefully curled against her temples.

"I appreciate your family taking me in," I said, bowing politely, "but our house was no shack. It was quite nice, and we had a garden, too. I helped my mother tend it."

"You . . . tended your own garden?" Miss Willow's mouth twitched, almost as if she were fighting a smirk.

I guess proper young ladies did not soil their hands.

I shifted my feet uncomfortably. "If we didn't do it, there was no one else to keep the garden alive."

"But . . . to dirty your hands that way." Miss Willow pantomimed digging with pale, exquisitely manicured fingers. "Where all the bugs are."

"But it's so nice to sit in a garden," I said, puzzled. That was, after all, what a garden was for.

"Do I look like a water buffalo?" Miss Willow laughed as she fluttered a mother-of-pearl fan. "The only plants I want to see are carved out of huge lumps of jade."

"Willow, we must make allowances," Miss Emerald gently scolded her sister. "There's been no one to show her the proper way."

"At least we won't have to teach her how to dress. Wherever did you get such exquisite clothes?" The envy was plain in Miss Willow's voice.

It made me feel proud to find that a rich girl with such fine clothes would want my mother's handiwork.

"My mother made them for me," I explained proudly.

Miss Emerald pretended to pout sadly. "But somehow

we really must increase those cuffs to the floor. Perhaps a black satin border."

I stared down at my trousers. "I've seen plenty of girls with pants this length."

"Yes, my dear, but your feet are . . ." Miss Emerald leaned forward to whisper, "How shall I put this? Rather . . . um . . . large." She scrunched up her face as if she had just bitten into a slice of bitter melon.

"They're only a little larger than yours," I countered.

It was the fashion among rich Chinese families to bind a girl's feet because it made them more attractive. Using ribbons, they bent a young girl's toes under the sole to shape the feet and keep them small. Bound feet were considered desirable, but they made it hard to walk.

Miss Emerald slid her own feet underneath her chair as if she were embarrassed. "It's our mother, I'm afraid. She's half Hakka, and they don't do that to their girls."

The Hakka were a large group from another province that had kept their own language and own customs when the Manchus moved them here. For several years now, the locals had been fighting a war to exterminate them.

"Is your mother Hakka too?" Miss Oriole asked me.

"No," I said. "My mother's feet were bound, and it was so painful, she vowed she would never do it to her daughter. It didn't stop her from working in the garden, though."

"Mothers," Miss Emerald sighed. "They just don't understand what we're going through."

"Actually, I'm grateful," I insisted proudly.

"You'll learn fast enough when the other girls make fun of you," Miss Willow said smugly.

"No doubt," I said, "but I won't change a thing about either my feet or my trousers."

Miss Emerald raised her hands as if she had tried her best to help me. "At least let us do something about your hair. Whatever will people say if we let you run around like that?"

I felt myself blushing as I touched my braids, which hung down my back. Perhaps in digging up the camellia, some earth had specked my hair somehow. "Did I get dirt on me?"

She bit her lip. "No, no, my dear. But—"

"Girls haven't worn their hair like that in years," Miss Willow said bluntly.

I stroked one of my braids. "I suppose I kept doing it the way my mother showed me."

"A river rat in fancy clothes is still a river rat," Miss Willow sniffed.

"Willow, she's our guest," Miss Emerald gently reminded her sister.

Miss Willow slumped sullenly in her chair. "People will still associate her with us."

It sounded as if the Sung sisters had been teased so much about their own unfashionable feet that they tried to be more stylish in everything else. They were like peacocks, trying to make up for their ugly feet by displaying the biggest and fanciest tails.

Miss Emerald studied me from several angles. "Oh, dear, but your hair's such a tangle. Do you ever break the teeth of your combs?"

I know Miss Emerald was only trying to help me, but in some ways her kindness was crueler than Miss Willow's contempt.

"Well, I think your hair and feet look pretty," Miss Oriole suddenly defended me.

Miss Emerald reached over from her chair to tap her youngest sister on the head. "Mind your elders, my darling."

Miss Oriole sat back, rubbing the spot where she had been hit. "Wisdom's supposed to come with age."

"And don't I protect you?" Miss Emerald said smugly. "You would have gone to the Lees' party in *last year's* shoes."

Miss Oriole dropped her chin down. "Yes," she admitted ruefully.

"You would have been the laughing stock of Canton," Miss Willow added.

Miss Oriole sat deflated in her chair for a moment, and then roused herself. "And I already thanked you a thousand times. Do you have to keep bringing it up?"

I stood patiently, waiting for a lull in the argument to ask, "Someone is having a party at a time like this?"

"What else is there to do?" Miss Willow asked.

I felt as if I had suddenly flown to the moon. "But there's a war on," I pointed out.

Miss Willow pressed her fan to her lips. "You don't mean to say you're afraid of the foreign barbarians?" she laughed. "Our troops sent them packing quick enough."

"Especially that dashing lieutenant from the Manchu regiment," Miss Emerald sighed.

"The only reason the British left last time was because there weren't enough of them. They'll come back with more ships and troops," I warned.

Miss Willow waved her fan as if she could blow the British and French ships back to their homeland. "And this time the viceroy and our brave officers will make those wretched barbarians beg for peace."

"But the foreigners have modern weapons," I argued, "not old muskets." I thought of what kindly Mr. Fortescue had told us. "Our weapons were fine for fighting a war two centuries ago."

They looked at me as if I were an annoying mosquito that had buzzed into the room.

"There's no way that Heaven would let them win," Miss Oriole insisted. "They're fighting a war so they can sell the opium they get from India here."

"Yes, their cause is unjust. But Heaven has already let them win one war just so they could flood the empire with their drugs," I said.

"Our empire is over four thousand years old," Miss Emerald argued. "How old are their kingdoms? A few hundred years?"

I tried to reason with them, but it was no use. Their tongues were sharp enough, so I knew their minds had to match, but the two older girls took no more interest in the outside world than birds in a cage. What concerned them was what happened inside their own mansion and those of their friends.

Miss Oriole wanted to discuss things, but only to be reassured that her home would be safe, whatever happened.

I had been wrong. The Sung mansion was not a prison. It was some fairy grotto where time and life follow rules separate from the real world of Canton.

And now I was trapped inside.

4 *The Test*

I was grateful when Snow Goose came back and sullenly announced, "The Master and Mistress will receive you now."

"If you'll excuse me," I said, nodding to the girls. Miss Emerald and Miss Willow were deep into the merits and demerits of damask silk. Only Miss Oriole smiled in acknowledgment.

Snow Goose led me around the overgrown garden to the center of the mansion. "How do you ever find your way around?" I asked her.

"You learn," the maid shrugged, "or you get lost and starve to death." It was hard to tell from her back if she was joking or serious.

About ten feet from an ornate doorway, her posture changed. She stood straighter and she took smaller, daintier steps. It was like watching an actor assume a role. Tapping at the door, she waited demurely until a voice said, "Enter."

When she opened the door, she transformed like an actor on the stage. Vanished was the sullen, insolent girl, and in her place was the very picture of meekness.

"The Master will see you now," Snow Goose informed me with a deep bow. She was putting on quite a show for her master.

Even with my eyes closed, I would have known it was a study by the familiar smell of scented ink. Elegant teak cabinets with fancy brass fittings held piles of books. Another cabinet held shelves of snuff bottles, and the walls were adorned with scrolls written in different beautiful hands. On tables scattered around the room were strange-shaped rocks on thin, long-legged stands. An antique sword hung near one corner.

The teak desk's intricate carvings had literary themes. One side showed a poet trying to embrace the moon's reflection upon a lake. Another side showed poets drinking wine and writing poems in a pavilion on a mountainside.

On the desktop itself were a scholar's tools. Father's had been of cheap wood or stone, but from the inkwell to the cylinder that held the brushes, Master Sung's were of precious jade. I was sure the brushes' hairs were of the finest quality.

Behind the desk sat a familiar face, for Master Sung had often visited my father. "Spring Pearl, it's so nice to see you again. I'm just sorry that the occasion is so unhappy." He shook his head sadly. "Such a great loss to the world of art and literature."

He wore the cap of a scholar, but his robe was of a costly silk brocade that most scholars could not afford. He was a short barrel of a man with the same ink-stained fingers as my father. Turning, he introduced the tall woman sitting beside him. "This is my wife, Mistress Sung."

She was taller than her husband, had pale skin, and looked as if she had stepped out of a portrait of an empress. Her robe was of rich lavender brocade silk over a blue skirt, and her hair was wrapped around a wire frame into the shape of a butterfly's wings. From her rich, dark tresses hung little flowers of jade and coral.

Tilting back her head, she looked down her refined nose at me. "So," she said, "you are my husband's orphan."

Suddenly I remembered that I wasn't there on a tour of the mansion but that I was a charity case. Bowing my head gratefully, I slipped into formal speech. "I'm grateful for your kindness."

Master Sung waved a hand as if embarrassed. "It's the least I can do for the daughter of my great friend. Really, we should have had you visit long ago."

Mistress Sung, though, said nothing, but she appraised me with the same penetrating eyes as her daughters.

"I'll try not to impose any longer than I have to," I said nervously.

"Nonsense. Stay as long as you like," Master Sung said. He played with a stack of large, round silver coins, clinking them one after another. "Your father was always so gentle in critiquing my poor paintings and poems."

I couldn't help smiling. "He was always grateful to you for protecting him against classroom bullies when you were boys at school together."

Master Sung sighed. "My only talent in school, I'm afraid." He held up his hand with the coins. "The only other thing I'm good at is making money." He said it almost guiltily. "As they say, 'fragrant ink, stinking money.'"

I was trying not to be rude, but I was also curious. "I've never seen coins like those."

Master Sung held up one. "These are silver coins from *Mex-i-co*," he said, pronouncing the last word carefully. "They're replacing Chinese coins as currency."

I had seen silver coins like those at the Thirteen Factories, where they used them as currency with their Chinese customers. "Mex-i-co," I said, trying to remember what Father's foreign friends had said about that country. "I believe it is south of the Land of the Golden Mountain."

That was what everyone called America, where gold had been discovered eight years ago.

Mistress Sung spoke up for the first time. "You know a bit about other countries."

"We used to visit some of the foreign merchants

near . . . " I almost said "the riverside," but caught myself in time, ". . . our home."

Mistress Sung knew full well where I had lived. "Yes, the Rats' Nest would be convenient for that." Her tone made it clear that she, too, disapproved of my old neighborhood.

Master Sung was clinking the coins again anxiously. "And so you got to learn about the world. How marvelous!" He glanced at his wife as if to make a point.

I began to wonder if I was being examined—not by Master Sung, but by his wife. Was she judging if I was fit company for her daughters? I thought of their comments on my hair and the length of my cuffs. Was I going to be put out on the street because of them?

I knew that, even before this new war, there were many who despised foreigners and anyone who associated with them. But I saw nothing to be ashamed of.

"But it's all secondhand from her father," Mistress Sung said to her husband.

"I was able to ask my questions directly," I said proudly.

"You understand their *gobble-gobble* talk?" Mistress

Sung asked me skeptically.

"Enough," I admitted, "for simple conversations. They were so homesick that they loved to talk about their homes and their families and what life was like in their countries."

"Naturally, naturally," Master Sung nodded encouragingly. "I've always said foreigners are just like us."

"I've always found them so." I gave a start when I noticed one of Father's paintings on the wall behind their heads. I saw the strange, twisted tower-like crags that were called the Seven Stars.

Master Sung jingled the coins, pleased that I had noticed the painting. "You recognize my treasure!"

"Yes, I remember the day Father painted it. He had his sketches all over one wall," I said. It was like meeting an old friend, and in my delight, I forgot my manners and walked over to it. "The garden was so sunny that month. He had me read poetry to him while he painted."

Mistress Sung gazed at me skeptically. "You can read?"

I reminded myself to be polite and slipped back into

formal conversation. "I tried my best, but I could only learn a little of my father's knowledge."

"Then will you be so kind as to read this," Mistress Sung said and shoved a thick book over to me.

I picked up the book, recognizing it as a collection of poetry by a poet who lived a thousand years ago. "Where would you like me to begin?"

"Or, if you would like something simpler . . ." Master Sung suggested nervously.

"We agreed it should be something difficult," Mistress Sung sniffed.

"Yes," Master Sung said unhappily, but he kept his peace.

"Just read wherever you want," Mistress Sung said and sat back as if expecting me to fail.

Father had once told me that some philosophers believe nothing happens by chance. Everything is destined, and everything is interconnected. By throwing coins, the pattern that emerges will tell the future. So I simply opened the book and looked at a poem. It was full of archaic characters with many strokes, but I remembered having read this one with Father.

Lonely is the moon
And lost is my soul
Until I join you soon.

Master Sung slapped his hand on the desk in delight. "She's a regular scholar. Not even our son could do that."

"Another," Mistress Sung said.

The next poem was new to me, but I recognized many of the characters, so I read it as best I could, telling them truthfully when I did not know a word.

"I wonder if Blessing's tutor could do even that much," Master Sung crowed. "And he passed the first of the government exams."

Mistress Sung, though, kept to the point. "And you can write?"

"I have a tolerable hand," I said modestly. Actually, Father had exhibited my calligraphy. "I used to help my father write letters for people."

"You copied them from form letters in a book?" Mistress Sung asked.

"Sometimes," I nodded, "but in special cases, I had

to compose them myself."

"Our guest is quite accomplished," Master Sung declared triumphantly to his wife.

Mistress Sung inclined her head ever so slightly as she conceded that point. "Still, I'm sure our guest will want to be useful."

Master Sung hemmed and hawed. "Oh, really, my dear, I don't think that's necessary."

"So you've said," Mistress Sung sighed.

I thought of the Sung sisters, and I shuddered inside at the idea of being locked up like a bird in a cage. "But I would like to help."

"You see," Mistress Sung said to her husband.

Master Sung nodded to me. "You really do not have to do this."

"Thank you," I said with a bow, "but I'm not used to being idle."

Mistress Sung laced her fingers together and peered at me over her fingertips. "What the household requires is a seamstress. I understand your mother sewed."

"That's an insult to her mother. She was a magician with a needle!" Master Sung interrupted. "That's like

saying her father messed up paper with spots of color."
He waved a hand at the painting.

Mistress Sung, though, ignored her husband. "So
you can sew as well as you read and write?"

"I tried to learn," I confessed, "but I'm terrible at it."
My mother had tried to teach me in her gentle
manner, but I was hopeless. I had stuck my fingers
with needles more times than I cared to remember.

"You were raised to be more of a son than a daughter,"
Mistress Sung said bluntly.

"My dear," Master Sung said, shocked at his wife's
rudeness.

"I'm afraid there is some truth to that," I admitted.

"She'll be of small use to the household," Mistress
Sung countered.

"I could do simple repairs," I offered. "And I could
tend the garden."

"We don't have any garden staff to follow your
orders," Mistress Sung sniffed.

Master Sung dipped his head apologetically. "The
taxes have been so heavy over the years, what with
trying to control the rebels."

As if China didn't have enough trouble with the foreigners, there were all sorts of rebels causing trouble, too. The worst was a mad Chinese man who had convinced himself that he was related to the foreigner's god, and had gathered a huge army of rebels called the T'ai-pings several years ago. As preposterous as his notions were, his revolt had spread into other parts of the empire now.

Master Sung spread his hands in frustration. "And of course, now we have to pay for fighting the British and the French. This war has been especially costly, you understand. And the foreign blockade is ruining trade. We can't afford to hire new help."

"I'm quite capable of handling the garden myself," I sympathized.

Unlike her daughters, the elegant Mistress Sung was horrified rather than amused. I might as well have confessed to stealing. "You dug in the dirt?" she asked, shocked.

"With my mother," I said, wondering if I'd just gotten myself expelled. But I went on, "I hate to see a garden going to waste."

"We may waste whatever we want," Mistress Sung said stiffly.

I realized that the Sungs' garden didn't mean the same thing to them that ours had to us. They had a garden not because they loved it, but because it was what every rich family had. It was simply an example of wealth—like their mansion and other luxuries.

"If her father allowed it, I see no reason why we can't," Master Sung shrugged.

"His eccentricities are well-known," Mistress Sung snapped. "He passed the government exams so high that he could have chosen any post he wanted. And yet he chose to live in that hovel."

"He was pure in the pursuit of his art," Master Sung insisted.

"If his wife hadn't sewed, they would have starved," Mistress Sung argued. "As it is, she died from overwork."

"I don't mean to be rude," I said politely—though it was Mistress Sung who had the poor manners, "but my parents chose the life they did. And they were quite happy." I added as a challenge, "How many can say that?"

Mistress Sung would not back down. "And they left you a poor orphan, depending upon the kindness of strangers."

I liked Master Sung, but not his wife and children. "Then I won't offend you any longer. I'll gather my things and leave."

"But what will you do?" Master Sung asked, worried.

I tilted my head up proudly. "I'll beg on the streets if I have to, but I won't live with people who say such things about my parents."

Master Sung twisted around to plead with his wife, "But we can't have that."

I don't think Mistress Sung was used to having people talk back to her and her husband. As she took in a deep breath, her nostrils widened. "We can't have her disrupting our household either." She looked as if she were staring at a balance that was weighing my value against all the trouble I could cause.

I shifted my feet uneasily. If the Sungs threw me out, I could go back to the Rats' Nest, I guess. But how would I make a living? No one would go to a girl to write letters. I'd wind up begging, just as I said. If I had to become a beggar, though, I wouldn't begin here with Mistress Sung—not after the things she had said about my parents.

Master Sung began to fidget in his chair and I started to think about finding Doggy and getting my baskets when Mistress Sung finally reached a decision. "We would be quite within our rights to turn you out this moment," she informed me. "But I see some promise in you. And, after all, your parents were not without some reputation. It's a question of trimming and straightening a bit."

Master Sung breathed a sigh of relief. "So she can stay?"

Mistress Sung dipped her head reluctantly. "For now. She can earn her keep sewing. Don't you think so?" Though it was phrased like a question, it was clearly an order.

Master Sung nodded his head eagerly. "Yes, my dear, your advice is always so helpful." Then, beaming, he turned to me. "Welcome to the House of Sung, child. May you be as happy here as we are."

Or, I thought, *as happy as his wife and children would let me be.*

5 Pins and Needles

I followed Mistress Sung through the mansion to a small room filled with cabinets and a couple of narrow tables and waited in the doorway while she unlocked a cabinet door. "I think this color would look nice on Willow, don't you?" she asked, taking out a bolt of expensive blue silk.

"Miss Emerald knows so much more than I do. Maybe you should ask her," I said humbly.

Mistress Sung, though, gave me dimensions for a blouse. When she came back an hour later, she gazed in dismay at all the scraps on the table. "You wasted so much of the material," she said.

"I'm sorry," I said softly.

Her face was serious when she held up my attempt at a blouse. "This would be excellent—if Willow's left

arm were two meters long and her right half a meter."
She studied the stitches, which zigzagged everywhere.
"I don't see a straight stitch anywhere." She squinted
closer. "And is that blood?"

"I stabbed myself a couple of times with the needle."
I held up my fingers. I'd improvised bandages from
some rags. "I know I ruined that blouse. I'll work twice
as hard to make up for it."

Mistress Sung studied me thoughtfully and then
dropped the blouse into a basket of rags. "You can't
sew at all, can you?"

"My mother tried and tried to teach me," I confessed,
"but I could never get the knack of it. I'm hopeless."

"Well, we can't afford to waste silk while you learn,"
she said, and added, "if ever."

"Perhaps I could help with the mending," I offered.

"I think you need a bit more practice before we
let you do even that," Mistress Sung said tactfully.
"I know. When you aren't practicing your stitches,
you can help make shoes for the servants."

I stared at my bandaged fingertips and thought of
more wounds. "Perhaps I could help in the kitchen?"

I asked hopefully.

Mistress Sung looked hurt. "We aren't ogres, my dear. How could we make the daughter of a scholar stoop that low? I'll have Snow Goose show you how to make shoes."

Mistress Sung fetched Snow Goose, who came in and smirked all the while that she showed me how to paste clean scraps together to make a shoe's sole. However, since the scraps weren't all the same size, it was like fitting pieces of a puzzle together—and there were at least twenty layers of scraps. Eventually, the sole was attached to the cloth upper part of the shoe. It was hard to force the needle through so much cloth, even with a thimble. Once enough of the needle had pierced through the sole, I needed a special pair of wooden pliers to pull the needle through the rest of the way.

It was hard work that made my fingers ache. When I wasn't working on shoes, I practiced my stitches, because at the end of the day Mistress Sung was going to check them.

"Well, perhaps tomorrow you'll get the hang of it,"

Mistress Sung sighed. "Now wash up and get dressed. We dine in an hour."

I blinked. "I won't be eating with the servants?" After all, I was a charity case.

She looked at me as if I were a simpleton. "Don't be absurd. No matter how eccentric your father was, he was still a scholar. What would people say if you didn't dine with us?"

I tried to follow her directions to my room, but I wound up asking Snow Goose for help. I couldn't believe it was my bedroom at first, for it had a cabinet and chairs and a real four-poster bed instead of a sleeping mat. But then I overheard a servant in the hallway asking Snow Goose what to do with some old trash, and Snow Goose joked that they could put it in my room, along with the other old furniture.

I examined the furniture more closely and saw that it was still dusty because no one had bothered to clean it; and through the layers of dirt, I saw many scratches and nicks.

No matter what Master Sung said, it was clear what the rest of his household thought of me. Hoping to fit in, I tried to copy the hairstyle of one of the Sung sisters, but I soon gave up in despair. I couldn't imitate even Miss Oriole's simple one. As I twisted my hair into my usual braids, I felt even more alone.

But then my eye caught sight of my belongings in a corner. Doggy had carefully placed my camellia plant on top of them. I told myself it was time to stop feeling miserable. I hated people who whined—especially if it was me. I might not be able to help myself, but at least I could do something for my flower.

Mistress Sung had not actually forbidden me to work in the garden, so after putting on a plain blouse and pants, I found my way there. I waded through the high weeds until I found a spot I thought the camellia would like.

Yanking out weeds by the handful, I cleared a space and dug a hole. The cool soil soothed the tips of my fingers, which still hurt from my attempts at sewing. When Mother was sick, she had always felt better if she could get out into the garden. She had said her plants were better than any medicine, and, as I worked, I began to feel them healing me as well.

Pausing for a brief rest, I began to see what a magnificent place this had been once. Lost among the weeds were rare maple trees, flowers, and even orchids that Mother had talked about but that we had seen only in pictures in books. They were slowly being strangled now.

It was a garden no one wanted. Just like me.

I had felt so helpless and useless when each of my parents had died. All I could do was sit and watch the life flow from them. But I could do something for the plants here. I barely had time to get water in a bucket from the well and give some to my camellia before I heard Snow Goose calling.

I'd completely lost track of the time. I washed my face and hands in the bucket and then ran back to my room and changed hastily. Of course, I only had the one good set of clothes to wear—which the sharp-eyed Miss Willow duly noted as soon as I sat down breathlessly at the dining table.

Master Sung was also there, since it was an informal meal. On a more formal occasion, he would have eaten separately with the male guests. He was as observant as his daughter. "From the exquisite craftsmanship, I'd say your mother did that," he said, picking up his chopsticks, which marked the moment when everyone could begin eating. "I hear the viceroy's wife treasures the robe she has with your mother's embroidery. And there are art collectors all over the city who would die for one piece of the edging."

Dinner swarmed with beef, chicken, pork, and fish dishes, each finer than the last. I made a point to eat daintily, afraid of spilling gravy on my clothes.

Unfortunately, each bite became a gamble because Master Sung wanted to discuss poetry or fiction or art with me, which made it hard to concentrate. It was almost as if he were more hungry for such talk than for food.

At first, I kept my answers brief because I did not want to hog the conversation, but then Miss Emerald patted my hand. "You don't have to be polite, Miss Pearl. Feel free to tell Father when you're bored."

I blinked in surprise. "But it's always interesting to talk about how much influence our hills had upon Su Tung P'o's poetry."

The girls stared at one another and then began to titter. "Maybe at *your* dinner table," Miss Willow said, "but at nobody else's."

It was the first inkling I had that other families did not discuss art and literature during their meals. "Oh," I said.

Master Sung pointed to his cap. "I am a scholar, you know."

Miss Emerald smiled tolerantly. "Father, everyone knows that you *bought* that title because it carries all sorts of privileges."

"Like living in the Old City," Miss Willow added.

Master Sung shifted uncomfortably in his chair. "My title is not an empty one."

I could see, though, that his daughters' comments bothered him, so I tried to defend him. "My father said that Master Sung is one of the most learned men in the city. He would have passed the government exams at the highest levels."

"Girls, that's enough," Mistress Sung said. And at her chilly frown, we all fell silent.

Poor Master Sung sighed. "Thank you, Pearl, for

indulging a fledgling scholar. This money-grubber likes to pretend he's a man of letters sometimes."

Miss Emerald raised her eyes skyward. "Thank Heaven that Father's finally found someone to talk that dusty rubbish with." However, I don't think she regarded it as a virtue in me.

We had almost finished dinner when Blessing, the Sungs' only son and heir, swaggered in. Following the latest rage, little gold dragons hung from his hair, which had been braided into a queue. He was sixteen and quite handsome—and looked as if he knew it.

From Mistress Sung's indulgent smile, I could tell he was her favorite. "I'll have Cook fix something fresh for you."

"No need," Blessing said, sitting down. "I had dinner with some of my classmates at a restaurant." Even without the announcement, I would have known that from the many stains that ruined his expensive robe.

"You didn't pick up the bill again, did you?" Master Sung huffed.

Blessing slouched in the chair. "You don't want my friends to think I'm cheap, do you?"

"I don't want you frittering away your inheritance," Master Sung frowned.

"Now, now," Mistress Sung soothed, "*his* reputation is *your* reputation; if people see him being stingy, they'll say it's because business is bad."

"Business *is* bad," Master Sung insisted, "during this blasted war, and the British blockade is strangling what's left."

Though he had already eaten, Blessing picked up his chopsticks and began to fish morsels from the plates. "The war ought to be over soon. The viceroy already drove off the barbarians once. If they come back again, he'll beat them the same way he did the rebels."

"Which we're still paying for," Master Sung complained. "And on top of that, we have to pay—"

"—for fighting the British and French. These taxes are draining the life from us." Blessing mimicked his father's voice as he waved a fist in the air. Lowering it, he resumed his normal tone. "We've heard it a hundred times, Father."

"A thousand," Miss Emerald added.

Master Sung looked around the table at all his

children. "Then why doesn't it sink in? You cannot go on spending money on new fans and clothes and big banquets."

Blessing sullenly clicked the tips of his chopsticks together. "And if I lose my friends, with whom am I supposed to play chess?"

"I wish you were as passionate about your studies as you are about games," Master Sung said and then glanced at me. "But as I recall, Pearl, you were fairly good at chess."

"I usually lost," I confessed.

Blessing stared at me. "And who are you?"

"Chou Spring Pearl," I said with a respectful nod.

Blessing perked up. "I'll take it easy on you. Let's have a game."

As he started to rise, Mistress Sung reminded him gently, "When dinner is over."

Blessing sat back down quickly. "That's what I meant."

No one could leave the table until Master Sung was finished. He set his chopsticks over the mouth of his rice bowl as a sign that the meal was ended.

"Then let's go," he said.

The Sungs had a huge room that they used for formal dinners, but they took their private meals in a smaller, more informal room—I say smaller, but this one room alone was several times larger than my old home. The room next to it was used for their entertainment in the evening.

The chairs and sofas here were covered with comfortable cushions, and the tables had a variety of games, books, and musical instruments for the family's amusement. It was soon obvious that the Sung sisters were quite talented in their own right. The two older girls could play the lute and flute quite well, and Miss Oriole sang in a sweet little voice.

Mistress Sung picked up some embroidery from a chair and began to work on it, while Blessing led me over to a table where a chess set sat ready. I was used to a chessboard of paper with wooden disks for pieces, but the Sungs' board was of carved wood and the disks were of fine, painted porcelain with the names done in an elegant hand.

"I'm afraid I don't see your book, dear," Mistress

Sung said, glancing around.

"I don't feel like reading tonight anyway," Master Sung chuckled as he sat down beside me.

"No fair coaching the guest girl," Blessing warned.

"I wouldn't think of it," Master Sung said, folding his arms. "But let's say we spice it up a little with a wager."

"All right," Blessing grinned. "If she wins, I'll eat at home for a week. But if she loses, I get to treat nine friends to any restaurant I want."

"Done," Master Sung nodded.

Blessing, who claimed the first move, attacked right away, but he was all offense and no defense. It was easy to slip behind his attacking chariots and cannon, cross the river, and take his general.

Blessing stared in disbelief. "I've never gotten beat that fast."

Master Sung laughed. "You lasted longer than I did."

Blessing drew his eyebrows together suspiciously and looked at me. "You said you usually lost."

"To her father," Master Sung said, wiping an amused tear from his eyes. "He was a master at the game. But his daughter could always beat me."

"She got lucky," Blessing insisted and started to set the pieces up again. "Double or nothing."

"Done," Master Sung grinned.

Miss Oriole, though, had been watching. "I'll bet you my tortoiseshell comb against your ivory fan," she dared her brother.

"You'll be sorry," Blessing warned.

"I trust Miss Ratty," Miss Oriole declared.

The second game lasted longer but ended with the same result. When Blessing lost a third time, he turned and picked up a wooden box. "How is the guest girl at dominoes?" he asked his father.

Master Sung shook his head. "I never played with her."

"I'm terrible," I informed him. I didn't add that I usually played against gamblers who did it professionally in the wine shops. Of course, when I challenged them, we always used pebbles for the stakes, rather than money.

Miss Oriole, though, made another side bet with her brother, this time, for a beautiful and expensive mother-of-pearl box.

When I defeated him even at dominoes, his two other sisters settled in like vultures waiting for the kill and began wagering with him as well.

Though I won at dominoes two more times, Blessing just would not accept defeat and would have tried a fourth time. Depending on your view, he was either very determined or very reckless.

It was Master Sung who saved him. "I think you've met your match, boy. Why don't you stop?"

Blessing pretended to yawn. "I guess I'm more tired than I thought. I should never have played. But tomorrow night, I am going to find something I can beat you at."

"And until you do, Spring Pearl is going to save me a fortune," Master Sung said, with immense satisfaction.

"And we'll strip him clean," Miss Willow said, rubbing her hands together gleefully.

6 Miss Weed

Over the next week, Blessing kept trying to beat me at something—from cards to rock-paper-scissors to *mah jong*. However, as defeat piled up upon defeat, even he began to laugh about it.

"You're not mad at me?" I asked, surprised.

He shrugged good-naturedly. "I can never keep at anything for very long."

"Especially your studies," Master Sung sighed.

"One week something is his favorite delight, and the next week," Miss Willow pantomimed throwing something over her shoulder, "it's in the rubbish."

"Do I look like a drudge?" Blessing gave me an easy-going smile. "Books, amusements, friends, or grudges—anything gets boring if you stay fixed on it all the time."

"You never keep at anything too long because it smacks too much of work," Miss Willow teased.

Although he became friendly enough, his challenges became tiresome. I even thought about slipping him the loaded dice the gamblers had given me so he could win for once. The only refuge I had in the daytime was to retreat to my sewing. I heard from the servants that he spent all his time preparing for that evening's games rather than studying, as his father suggested.

His sisters were another matter. They didn't intend to be cruel—in fact, quite the opposite. After my first triumphs over their brother, they took a liking to me—unfortunately. The three sisters announced that they would transform me. Miss Willow even gave me one of her old outfits.

Whenever they tried to improve me, they meant to be kind. But none of the girls had a drop of sensitivity. In their suggestions about my hair, my clothes, and my manners, they never let me forget that I was "Miss Ratty." Though I tried my best not to show it, they hurt me deeply inside.

The days went by, but I never felt like one of them—I was only a sad creature who had been rescued from the slums. Even the servants took their cues from the children. They stopped being outright insulting and patronized me instead, constantly calling me "Miss Ratty."

My ears burned, and I longed to be back by the riverbank. My fellow Rats might be ragged and crude, but their kindness had no edge to wound.

The only truly friendly face was Doggy's. As he helped me hang my father's painting, he hummed cheerfully.

"I hate to spoil your mood," I apologized, "but I think the painting would be better over there." I pointed to a different spot.

I waited for the protest but, after stepping back and

examining his work, he nodded. "Right you are."

"Why are you so cheerful this morning?" I asked, curious. "Everyone else is complaining about the economizing."

Because of the British blockade and the increased war taxes, Master Sung had decreed that the household would have to cut its overall spending. Even the servants had begun to worry. Their wages had been reduced as well, and some had begun to fear losing their positions.

As Doggy began to put my father's painting in the new spot, he smiled. "Oh, I'm hurting too, Miss. My salary was low enough before the cuts that a bug would have tripped over it."

"Then what are you so happy about?" I asked. A new thought occurred to me. "I hope whatever scheme you've hatched is legal."

"Well, it's not that *illegal*," he said, adjusting the painting carefully. "And if it turns out the way I hope, I'll be joining my uncle when he sets up his company."

I was sure I knew his plans now. "I didn't think you would be the kind to take advantage of other people's suffering. Are you smuggling contraband?"

Doggy scratched his head, embarrassed. "I'm no smuggler, Miss. But I guess you could say I *am* profiting from someone's problems."

I frowned. "You disappoint me, Doggy."

"But you haven't disappointed me, Miss," Doggy said with a sly grin. "Everyone else bet against you, but right on that first day I bet my money on you."

I folded my arms and demanded, "To do what?"

Doggy chuckled. "Why, to stay, Miss. All the other servants were sure the young Sungs would send you packing; but when I met you . . . well, it's like my granny always said, 'You pick a fighting rooster not by the size of his spurs but by his spirit.' So I wagered on you to stay."

I wasn't sure I liked the comparison. "Does your grandmother ever run out of proverbs?" I asked, annoyed.

"A wise woman is my granny," Doggy said cheerfully, "even if she is a terrible cook."

I sighed. "You haven't won yet."

"Begging your pardon, but that's where you're

wrong, Miss," he winked. "Half of them thought you wouldn't last a day, so I've already been collecting."

"And the other half?" I wondered.

"I'll collect soon," Doggy grinned. "Just stick it out another month if you can. You're better than a prize fighting rooster."

As odd as the compliment was, it was the only one I had received in a long time. But I couldn't help scolding him. "Do you think it's fair to take your winnings from people who have had their salary reduced?"

Doggy rolled his eyes. "Oh, now, don't go getting all moral on me, Miss. They would have just as soon done the same to me."

A new thought had occurred to me. The Sung girls were friendly to me only after I had won them half of Blessing's things. Had I bought Doggy's friendship as well? "Is that the only reason you've been friendly to me? To encourage me so that you can win your bets?"

"Now, now, Miss," Doggy scolded, "you ought to know by now we servants aren't allowed to think anything." He added with a respectful nod, "But even if you had lost me all my wagers, I'd still think well of you. You're not like the young Sungs—that you're not."

"Then I'll do my best," I promised sourly, "to make you wealthy."

He opened his mouth to say something but then seemed to think better of it. "Thank you, Miss," was all he said, and with a bow, he started to limp away.

"Did you hurt your foot?" I asked.

"In a manner of speaking, Miss," Doggy said. "I'm wearing a pair of shoes you made. One of the soles is kind of lumpy."

"I'm sorry," I said.

"One of these years, you'll get the hang of it," he said, and left.

I gazed at my father's painting of junks and foreign ships floating along the river in front of the garden at the foreign factories. It usually brought me a sense of peace to remember my visits there with him. Today, however, I could not shake off the sense of loneliness. There was no one in the household whom I trusted anymore. And despite Doggy's fine words, I felt more like a prize fighting rooster than not. He felt affection only because I won wagers for him.

And right now I was a novelty to the Sungs. But when would Master Sung tire of talking to me? Or when would the fickle Blessing decide to find some other amusement? Would I be discarded like one of his fans?

I thought guiltily of the basket of rags in the sewing room, waiting to be made into shoes. It wasn't as if the wearers wanted them. With their wages cut, they had no choice.

I had been thinking of Doggy as my only friend in the Sung household. Now it seemed that he had only been kind to me because I was valuable to him. He was no better than the Sung sisters.

I couldn't see sitting and brooding in my room. It would only make me as sullen and unpleasant as the maid, Snow Goose. It was better to do something. At least with the garden, I was beginning to see some results.

So, putting on an old blouse and trousers, I went there now. I had been weeding and pruning in what little spare time I had. Plants are simpler than people: show them some kindness, and they respond in turn.

Of course, the Sung girls couldn't let my gardening pass. They teased me, saying that they had wanted to make me into a flower, but I was determined to be a weed. They stopped calling me "Miss Ratty" and began referring to me as "Miss Weed." Even Blessing started to call me that so often that I sometimes longed for my old nickname. However, I refused to let the taunts stop me.

There was so much more to work with in the Sungs' garden than in my old one at home. However, that meant more challenges, too, so I hardly knew where to begin. Mother had known how to design a garden so that it not only pleased the eye but also followed the rules of *feng shui*, the study of wind and water that harmonized a place with Nature. She could align the flowers and trees and shrubs for the best flow of energy, and she even knew when to plant by the phases of the moon. But I had never learned any of that, so all I could do was clear out the weeds and do my best for the survivors of the original plants.

Closing my eyes, I listened to the breeze rustling the plants and sniffed the many scents as the garden embraced me. At peace again now, I turned my face toward the sun like a flower, feeling the warmth bathe my eyes and cheeks. In my mind, I tried to pretend I was in my mother's garden. The mansion wouldn't let me, though. There were strange sounds, strange voices, and strange smells, so try as I might, I couldn't feel as if I were there.

Suddenly I heard Master Sung complaining, "These taxes are intolerable. And for what? For an attack that never comes."

"Yes, the British won't come back again," another man agreed. He was one of a dozen men in robes as elegant as Master Sung's. "They're too busy putting down that rebellion in their Indian colony."

"Lord Chin is right. Their whole empire is coming apart," a second man declared smugly. He looked the youngest, and was very handsome.

Lord Chin nodded. "What do you expect, Mister Ma, when an empire sells drugs?"

Master Sung spread out his arms dramatically. "Which is why I say we tell the viceroy that he will get nothing more from us."

"Pardon me, sir," I said, "but the British will come."
Instantly, I regretted my words as all their eyes swung
toward me. Too late, I realized I must look a fright.
My face was all sweaty, my hair was falling down, and
my blouse was covered in dirt.

Master Sung broke off his conversation with another
man. "Oh, it's you, Spring Pearl. What are you doing
here?"

I waved a handful of weeds at the garden. "I hated
to see the garden so neglected, so I thought I'd do
something about it."

"Well, get out of there," he snapped. He lost his
temper easily these days, but I didn't blame him at all.
"You're not a peasant."

"I'm sorry," I said, getting up.

"Have times gotten so bad for you that you're letting
anyone weed your garden?" the first man laughed.

"This is Master Chou's daughter," Master Sung said.
"Really, we treat her well. I don't know what possessed
her to play in the dirt."

I felt my cheeks blushing as the men all turned to
study me now.

"Don't you collect his paintings?" Mister Ma asked Lord Chin.

"And his wife's embroidery," Lord Chin said. I saw pity in his eyes.

Master Sung was right: it was not the proper image for the daughter of a famous scholar. Dipping my head respectfully, I murmured, "If you'll excuse me." Placing the weeds in my basket, I tried to leave.

"Why are you saving the weeds?" Lord Chin asked.

"Cook asked me to save them for fuel for the stoves," I blurted out nervously. Too late, I realized my mistake.

Lord Chin smiled at Master Sung. "So even you have had to economize."

"I hope you haven't cut the kitchen budget too low." Mister Ma patted his stomach. "I've saved my appetite for this meal."

I expected Master Sung to explode because I had made him lose so much face before his friends. He simply laughed, though. "You don't find such thrift in modern girls nowadays, do you?"

Mister Ma clasped his hands behind his back. "A

regular old-fashioned girl, hey?"

"Not so old-fashioned," Master Sung said. "Master Chou raised her to be a scholar. If she were a boy, she could sit for the government exams."

"I once saw a parrot that could recite all of the Five Classics," Lord Chin said. "But it didn't understand a word."

"Well, since you're so clever," Mister Ma asked, "tell us why you think the British will come."

When I licked my lips, I could taste the grit that clung to them. "We knew the foreign merchants, my parents and I." I tilted my head back and repeated what Mr. Fortescue had said one evening. "One of them called the British 'bulldogs'—once they clamp their teeth onto something, they don't give it up."

"This merchant spoke Chinese that well?" Master Sung asked.

"And we learned his tongue," I said. "Father always wanted us to learn new things." In fact, I had learned to speak English better than Father and could even write it a bit.

"This British merchant—" Master Sung began.

"Master For-tes-cue," I supplied.

"Yes, Master For-tes-cue. I know him. He's a formidable man," Master Sung went on, "but he is only one man. You can hardly form a judgment of an entire people on the basis of one man."

As a reprimand, it was a gentle one, and I dipped my head in acknowledgment. "Yes, sir, but . . ."

"But what, child?" Mister Ma coaxed.

"But the other foreign merchants were just as determined," I said. "And the British won't forget the bounty the viceroy placed on their heads. British stragglers and even a small mail ship were attacked and their heads taken. They will never forgive that."

Master Sung only heard what he wanted to hear. "Don't worry so, Spring Pearl," he said, patting me on the shoulder. "The British will find Canton's a tougher nut to crack the second time round. We have new guns in the forts and many more troops in the city."

Lord Chin nodded. "We should begin." And he began to walk in the direction Master Sung indicated.

As he left, Mister Ma turned back and winked at me. "Be sure to pick plenty of weeds for the kitchen. I like my tea piping hot."

As they walked away, though, I heard Lord Chin say to Master Sung, "I fear you're going to have that poor little thing on your hands forever. Who's going to want to marry an odd creature like that?"

7 *The Power Behind the Throne*

I sat for a long time in the garden. "Poor little thing."
"Odd creature." The phrases whirled round and round
my mind. I was not only a weed but also a monster that
no one wanted.

I couldn't help touching my hair and then my shabby
clothes. I suppose Master Sung's friends would prefer
someone like Miss Emerald. But it wasn't in me to be
pampered, like a little pet.

To my annoyance, I felt tears beginning to sting the
corners of my eyes. If there was one thing I hated, it
was self-pity. Though the weeds were a blur, I started to
dig, hoping I was rooting out the right ones.

There was a particularly tough patch of broad-leafed
weeds with tiny greenish-white flowers that grew knee-
high. I was tugging at one when I heard a door open

from a room on the side. I didn't look up.

"You're pulling out a very useful plant," Mistress Sung said.

Quickly I stopped pulling and bowed my head. "Good afternoon."

I watched uneasily as she walked toward me, sure that I would receive a lecture on how I was shaming my father. I knew what she and her daughters thought of digging in the dirt.

Instead, though, she squatted beside me. "That's called 'fragrant tiger bones.'" Taking part of it, she crushed the plant between her hands and then held out a palm for me to smell. It was a pungent but not unpleasant odor. "Country folk use it for mosquito bites and even sunburn. It's a very tough, hardy plant that can survive in many places where other plants cannot. Another name for it is 'goosefoot.'"

"Oh," I said, bracing for her to scold me about gardening without her permission.

However, Mistress Sung turned and cupped the camellia plant between her fingertips. "I was wondering who had been improving the garden. Did you plant this, Spring Pearl?"

"You didn't say that I couldn't," I said hastily. "I mean . . . I hope it's all right. I know it's common, but . . ." I hastily wiped my sleeve across my face. "I didn't ask for your leave. I'm sorry."

Mistress Sung smiled. "You're only smearing mud on your face now."

Master Sung's friends were right: I was a freak. Feeling miserable, I said, "I'll go clean up." And perhaps I would hide in my room for the rest of my life.

Mistress Sung put a hand on my shoulder to hold me in place. "In a moment. I couldn't help overhearing our visitors. Don't pay them any mind. When I was your age, people used to say it was a shame that I had been born a girl."

I listened to her round, polished tones and accents in utter amazement. She seemed so . . . elegant. "They did?"

Mistress Sung nodded. "Here's something my father told me once: 'A weed is a plant that hasn't found its home yet.' Let a seed blow into a rice field, and it's a nuisance that the farmer plucks out. But let that same seed blow into an herb garden, and that same farmer will be happy with it."

"Your father was a farmer?" I asked, astonished. "I thought your family were gentlemen and ladies for generations."

She gestured toward herself with a laugh. "My dear, you are gazing upon a girl who once had mud between her toes. But I was determined to be a wife Master Sung could be proud of, so I learned a few things."

I bit my lip for a long time as I digested everything she had told me. Finally, I said, "The goosefoot might be good as a border for some of the flowers. Maybe I'll shift it to someplace else, since it's useful after all."

"Yes," she agreed, brushing off the goosefoot bits that clung to her fingertips, "you merely have to find the right spot for it."

And, I thought, for myself. Perhaps I was an odd creature here, but surely there was a place for me somewhere. "And if you'll teach me the recipe for the insect-bite ointment, I'll try to make some."

"I'll do that. It always worked better than any new-fangled ointment the doctor gave us." She inhaled deeply. "I'd forgotten how sweet the scent of flowers can be. It's so much nicer than incense or perfume." She looked around. "I should come out here more often."

"I'll try to make it even better," I promised.

She glanced at me and then stared at the goosefoot as the top nodded in the breeze, waving the little flowers like bubbles. "I might have been a little cool when you first came here, but you have to understand why. My husband's scholarly friends are always taking advantage of him. They are constantly borrowing money and never paying it back. He has accomplished so much, and yet he still feels bad that they passed their exams and he never had the opportunity to."

"But Master Sung has become such an important man," I said.

"That's what I tell him all the time." She nodded, then made a face. "The title of 'Scholar' is the only success that some of those leeches have had in their entire lives; yet they lord it over my husband and never let him forget he bought his title. And so when you came—"

"—you thought I was another leech," I finished. She had only been trying to protect her husband. "I guess I have been pretty useless."

Mistress Sung stood up. "I have to say that your sewing is atrocious. Your shoes have maimed half our staff."

"I'll get better with practice, Mistress," I promised.

Mistress Sung clasped her hands behind her back. "I seriously doubt that. I can see how hard you try because your fingers are always bleeding, and yet you've made no improvement. However, now that my husband is organizing this tax protest, what he really needs is another clerk—only with so many people in the household, we don't have the budget for a new one."

It was what I was afraid of: with one less mouth to feed, they might be able to hire another clerk.

I felt like my heart had dropped right to my feet. "I see," I said softly. Finally, I understood the point of her proverb. I was the weed that needed to find the right home—somewhere else. "I'm grateful for all your hospitality, and I'll pack immediately and leave."

Mistress Sung looked puzzled. "Why? I just want you

to help with the correspondence. Some of it is rather confidential, and I would feel more comfortable if it was you and not a stranger."

I blinked. "You mean, write letters?"

"I believe that's what you said you did for your father," Mistress Sung said and gave a chuckle. "And it would also spare our staff's feet."

I was grateful not only for being allowed to stay but also for being freed from sewing. "My mother was a patient teacher, but I never got the knack."

"I have never seen anybody more determined and yet more inept with a needle. Your shoes had the kitchen servants almost in tears," Mistress Sung admitted. "So as soon as you clean up, come to my husband's study. We must begin immediately."

"Yes, Mistress," I said and scrambled to my feet.

"I intend to work you hard," she warned me.

"I've never been afraid of that," I said.

When she smiled, little lines appeared around the corners of her eyes. "I can see that now. But when you have a moment to spare, you may continue on the garden. Only be sure to wear a hat. A daughter of a scholar should not be as tanned as a field hand."

"Yes, Mistress," I said as she left, feeling happier than I had felt since I had arrived. I might not be as elegant as Miss Emerald, but even a weed girl had her uses!

Feeling more confident, I went to the study after washing and changing. Mistress Sung seemed quite at home, sitting at her husband's desk—as if she had done this many times before. I was in the robe my mother had made for me.

"You really didn't need to dress up for this," she said.

"My other gown is dirty," I confessed.

Mistress Sung frowned. "You mean, we didn't have more robes made for you?" When I shook my head, she nodded to me. "Then your first clerical job is to make a note to have another made for you. The maids can get the silk from the storage room."

"But you told your daughters that they couldn't have new dresses," I said. "Wouldn't that make for hard feelings?"

"If I say so, even a Rat has a right to clothes," Mistress Sung said. So she had overheard all her daughters' and the housemaids' taunts. I was beginning to think there wasn't much she missed. She picked up a pile of letters. "Before we turn to the protest, let's start with this stack. Read me the first one."

Through the floor, I could hear the rumbling of Master Sung and his friends.

I hesitated. "Perhaps we should wait until you can ask Master Sung."

Mistress Sung smiled. "He won't mind. I often help my husband with his many business affairs. I am not stupid, even if I can neither read nor write."

"I didn't say you were, Mistress," I said hastily.

"But it must be our little secret," she added. "We have to respect my husband's face outside the study."

I glanced at the stack. "But if you can't read, how do you know it's about business?"

"My husband arranges the stacks in a certain order," Mistress Sung said. "I'm as much his business partner as I am his wife. We let the clerks in the office handle the more common things, but we deal with the more sensitive items up here."

I found the ink brush far more comfortable to my

hand than the needle; and as we worked our way through the letters and her replies, I soon realized just how shrewd Mistress Sung was. Her husband was wise to trust her with his affairs.

I think I had as much to learn from her as from my father. He wrote letters and painted portraits only to earn enough to tide us over while he concentrated on his art. Scholars were supposed to be above such ordinary things as money.

He had left it to Mother and me to manage the cash to buy our meager meals. At an early age, I had learned the value of a coin as much as I had learned the wisdom of the classics.

I thought I had understood the Sung household, but in the next month I realized how little I had really seen. A household has as many currents and eddies as a river. The children and the servants all formed different groups, which sometimes cooperated with one another but more often quarreled.

I had thought Master Sung was like an emperor who simply gave commands. However, with Mistress Sung's help, I saw that Master Sung was more like an acrobat trying to balance on a tall stack of chairs. He had to keep the household happy even on a lower budget— though what the Sungs considered a limited budget would have clothed and fed the entire Rats' Nest quite comfortably. And though Master Sung's official business was silk, he had his finger in many other dumplings. From his old files, I was also happy to learn that he liked to do business only with foreign merchants like Mr. Fortescue, who did not deal in opium.

Master Sung himself was occupied with the tax protest. Many of the merchants in the city were opposed to paying for a war that they were sure would never happen. He always seemed to be rushing to or returning from some meeting. That left most of the business matters to Mistress Sung. She soon taught me that it was as difficult to keep money as it was to make it.

As Doggy's granny had said, though, the nail that sticks out gets hammered, and Master Sung stuck out the most of all. So naturally, the government decided to smash him first.

8 *The Traitor*

The soldiers came in the night. At first, when I heard the shouting, I thought it was the Sung girls quarreling among themselves again. Then I realized that the voices were too deep and too numerous.

Bare feet thumped past me in the hallway as I went to the door. Maids were running this way and that like a flock of hens at the sight of Cook with a chopping knife. I grabbed Snow Goose. "What is it?"

She looked at me with wide, frightened eyes. "Thieves!"

Another maid skidded to a halt. "No, it's assassins."

There were as many opinions as there were maids, but none of them had seen anything themselves; they'd only heard the noise.

I stood there in exasperation when I heard weeping

coming from Miss Emerald's room. Worried, I knocked at the door, and when no one answered, I barged in. Over on the bed, I saw three shapes huddled together.

"Are you all right?" I asked them. "What's happened?"

"Oh, Miss Weed!" Miss Oriole exploded from the bed and darted toward me. Her tears wet my night-dress. "We're going to die."

Behind her, I saw Miss Willow anxiously biting at one corner of the quilt. Miss Emerald roused herself. "I . . . I should find out." I saw her rock back and forth as if she were trying to move, but she was so scared that her legs refused to respond.

I was feeling just as frightened, but then I thought of all the kindnesses that her parents had done me. Perhaps they would be sad if something happened to

The Last Flower

me, but they would grieve for their daughter. So it would be better for me to take the risk than her.

Besides, I felt sorry for the girls. The real world had just smashed their happy little fairy grotto. But I remembered to save her face. "Let me go. You should stay here to defend your sisters," I said. Glancing around the room, I saw a statue of a handy size. "Here. Take this."

With Miss Oriole still clinging to me, I grabbed the statue and took it over to Miss Emerald. As she took it, she looked up at me, embarrassed. "I should really be the one to go. After all, I guess I'm your host."

I felt some small satisfaction that she had realized it at last, so with a small grin I reassured her. "Rats are good at slipping in and out of tight places. I'll be all right." Then, freeing myself from Miss Oriole, I promised the little one, "I'll be right back."

After I had returned to my room to pull on some clothes, I made my way through the dark hallways filled with panicked servants. Fear filled the air like some evil, sickly incense, and I began to regret my decision.

However, before I could change my mind, I stumbled into the garden. Uniformed soldiers stood in the middle of it, heedless of the flowers. Some were armed with spears, others with lanterns.

In front of them was Lord Chin, reading from a proclamation. "'Whereas the accused has fomented treason—'"

Master Sung struggled to free himself from two burly soldiers. "But you were the loudest protester!"

"Only to draw out the traitors," Lord Chin explained.

Master Sung spat at Lord Chin, hitting him in the face. "You are the traitor! I thought you were my friend, and yet you've betrayed me."

Lord Chin signaled to a soldier, who struck Master Sung. Then, wiping off the spittle, Lord Chin droned on again, "'. . . the accused shall be interrogated and tried for high crimes against the empire.'" Lowering the proclamation, he nodded curtly to some other soldiers.

They stepped forward with a *cangue*, a wooden yoke that fits around a prisoner's neck.

Mistress Sung, her hair flowing down her shoulders, tried to shove them back. "How dare you treat my husband like a common criminal!"

"Then your husband must be an uncommon one," Lord Chin said.

When one of the soldiers pushed Mistress Sung to the ground, Master Sung was more concerned with his wife's welfare than his own. "Don't touch her!" he said and tried to leap forward.

However, his captors' grip was unbreakable.

"Let him go," Mistress Sung said, as she tried to rise.

I ran forward, afraid that the soldiers would hurt her if she continued to fight. "Mistress Sung, no," I said, and held onto her. "Think of your children."

"Yes, think of them," Master Sung ordered.

Mistress Sung stretched out a hand toward her husband, but she stayed in my arms.

Master Sung was a proud man, and though he tried to resist, one of the soldiers slowly forced his head down. The rectangular wooden collar fitted around his neck so that it looked like he had thrust his head through a small, legless table. On it was written in bold strokes: "Traitor." Once the yoke was locked in place, its weight forced him to bend over.

It made me want to weep like Mistress Sung to see him humbled that way.

"Good evening, Mistress Sung," Lord Chin said. "I'm sure we shall meet again." Raising a hand in salute, he climbed into a sedan chair. Instantly, the soldiers hoisted him into the air while a squad of soldiers pivoted and began to march out. Another squad fell into step behind, while more soldiers surrounded Master Sung.

As the kindly man stumbled forward, one of the soldiers prodded him with a spear butt. "Hurry it up there, fatty."

Mistress Sung bit her lip as she held onto me tightly.

"We haven't got all night," another said with a laugh as he, too, poked Master Sung.

"We'll have you free soon!" Mistress Sung promised.

Master Sung, though, shook his head. "Think of the children," he repeated.

"We'll all be here waiting when we get you out," his wife vowed.

He shambled out awkwardly as his escorts tormented him. Perhaps the worst torture would be to his pride, for he would be paraded through the streets that way. When the last lantern was gone, we were left in the dark garden.

Mistress Sung gazed up at the half moon, her hair falling into her face. "We must get help."

"Yes," I agreed, "and we must see that he has proper clothing and food. But we must also remember his command."

She squeezed me harder. "But the viceroy won't arrest the children, too."

Mistress Sung had been rich so long that she had forgotten the bitter truth that all poor folk know: mice don't walk up to cats and make demands. "When the legal machinery takes a prisoner, sometimes it chews up the family as well," I said. "I think he was warning you against charging in recklessly."

Mistress Sung shook her head as if trying to clear it. "And we have business enemies who would love to use this excuse to carve up our holdings."

"Even now?" I asked. "With the British at the gates?"

Mistress Sung let me go. "There are all sorts of wars and battles being fought."

"I've seen crabs at the fishmongers' trapped in a tub. Instead of trying to escape, they try to eat one another," I said thoughtfully.

"The crabs have nothing on humans," Mistress Sung said. "And . . . and then, what if he is convicted of treason—"

"You mustn't think that. He's done nothing wrong," I insisted.

Mistress Sung began to straighten up. "But if that happens, the viceroy can seize his assets."

Suddenly, I began to understand. "Which can then be distributed to the viceroy's friends."

Mistress Sung nodded. "Like Lord Chin." Now that she had something specific to focus on, she began brushing off her robe, as if the specks of dirt were the traitors. "We must protect as much as we can."

I watched her rise from the earth, tall and strong and proud. She was more of a warrior than any of the soldiers I had just seen.

"If I can be of any help," I said, "let me."

"I think," Mistress Sung said, "that I can find a few things for you to do. But first, spread the word that everyone—servants and family—is to gather in the reception hall."

It was a sorry, terrified bunch that collected in the large room. The chairs and tables had all been moved against the walls, so there was plenty of room to stand. I stood with the Sung girls, holding Miss Oriole's hand. I was surprised, though, that Miss Emerald and Miss Willow also pressed close to me, as if for reassurance.

The servants stood behind, but from glimpses over my shoulder, I saw they were as frightened as I was. The older ones were even crying, sure that the Sung household was now doomed. Only Doggy caught my eye and gave me an encouraging nod.

We all bowed when Blessing walked stiffly into the room, followed by his mother. He looked pale and he spoke woodenly, as if reciting a memorized speech. "These are sad times, but we will soon have my father free." His voice broke at that moment, and he choked back a sob. Shaking the tears from his eyes, he looked at us blankly until his mother whispered something to him. "In the meantime, my father expects you all to carry on your duties as if he were here. As his heir, I am now the head of the household until he returns."

Some of the servants began to weep even louder at the news—as if that only confirmed their belief in their doom. Though I liked Blessing, I had my own doubts about whether he could hold up under the pressure.

No one slept after that, least of all me. Instead, at Blessing's invitation, I joined him and his mother in his father's study. But he looked lost in the great mahogany chair.

I had to admire how tactful Mistress Sung was. She couched her orders in the form of suggestions and tactful questions that steered her son to the right course. Most of it involved protecting their business and property. Customers and creditors had to be reassured that things would go on just as before. Certain valuables would have to be hidden away, in case the worst happened. The titles to buildings and lands would have to be transferred in some way to protect them.

At first, Blessing seemed to enjoy it, as if it were a new game he was trying to master. At his mother's prompting, Blessing had sent out messengers to the other tax protesters, but one of them brought back bad news. "Mister Ma has been arrested, too."

I thought of that handsome, confident man. It was hard to picture him with his head bowed within a cangue.

If Viceroy Yeh had thought to frighten the other tax protesters, he had. All of them made some excuse or another why they could not come.

"Then we are alone," Mistress Sung said when she heard from the last of her messengers.

It was slowly dawning on Blessing that this was no game and that to lose meant disaster. "What are we going to do?" he said, his voice tightening with fear.

His mother was of a more practical mind. "First things first; we send some clothes to your father," she decided. "I had been hoping that one of his so-called friends would take clothing to him, but all of them are treating us like lepers."

She was missing the obvious choice—or perhaps

she was simply trying to spare me. I spoke up. "A servant might not be able to talk his way in, Mistress Sung," I said. "Let me go."

"I couldn't possibly," Mistress Sung said, and glanced at her son.

Blessing swallowed, "It's . . . it's my place, after all."

I could have wriggled off the hook, but I couldn't let Blessing go in my place. I owed that much to Master Sung for his many kindnesses. "But what if they decide to grab you as well? If they had you as a hostage, they could force your father to sign a confession," I pointed out. "Besides, you've never tried to talk Uncle Soo the butcher out of free bones for soup," I said. "If I can do that, I can talk my way into jail."

Mistress Sung studied me and then her son before she nodded. "Let's let Pearl try first." She thought a moment. "But we'll send a servant with you."

I thought of all the servants who might be a suitable escort, but there was really only one choice. "Perhaps Doggy."

Mistress Sung made a fist. "I was thinking of someone burlier and stronger."

My heart was beating fast. "To see Master Sung, I will need slyness, not muscle."

"Then Doggy it is," Mistress Sung said, and she turned to her son to plan what to say to the clerks when they came in a few hours to begin work.

9 *The Collector*

Before I went to change, I surveyed the garden quickly. I was appalled to see how much damage the soldiers had done, but at least they had spared the camellia.

Back in my room, I decided to put on my best clothes, since I was going to have to talk to officials. As I put on the jacket, I thought of my mother again. She had made each flower with such love. As the cool smoothness of the silk touched my skin, I felt as if she were holding me again. Silently I said a prayer to her and Father.

When I went into the outer courtyard, Doggy was waiting for me with a package under his arm. "I hear I have you to thank for this."

Though I felt as if we might be heading to our own

prison cell, it would never do to start a trip in such a gloomy frame of mind. So I forced myself to sound cheerful. "It's high time someone contributed to your education. Perhaps seeing what a jail is like will change your mind about cheating people."

"Oh, I know what jails are like." Doggy pointed at his feet so I could see the ragged, holey pair of shoes he was wearing. "You'll notice I'm wearing an old pair that you didn't make so I can run faster. As my granny says, 'A rabbit's feet may look funny, but it can run quick.'"

The streets were eerily empty. All the buildings had their doors locked and windows shuttered. Word of the arrests had already spread. Viceroy Yeh, it seemed, had made his point to the entire city.

The only sounds were of the soldiers drilling in the distance, still practicing to fight the British. On one of his visits, Mr. Fortescue had brought a hunting rifle to show us. It was a sleek, powerful weapon. He had said that the British army had arms many times better. What could our swords and old-fashioned muskets do against weapons like those?

"What do you think will happen when the British finally attack?" I asked Doggy.

He strolled along, apparently glad of the morning off from his regular duties. "They'll win like last time, of course. And then my uncle and me will have a chance."

I stared at him in horror. "How can you hope the British will win? They'll force us to let them keep on peddling their drugs here," I protested.

Doggy dipped his head apologetically. "They shouldn't sell opium. But they'll shake up some things. Before the last war, the empire made it impossible for regular folks like me to trade with the foreigners. Only a few Chinese merchants got rich. I bet the rules will loosen up even more after this new war is over."

He closed the fingers of his free hand into a tight fist. "This is the way things are now. Everything is locked in place. Master Sung and his family are on top." He held up his thumb. "And I'm stuck on the bottom." He extended a pinkie. "But when the British come back, that will all change." Opening his hand again, he wriggled all his fingers. "And folks like me and my uncle'll be on the same level as Master Sung."

I stepped over a puddle, careful not to muddy my trouser cuffs. "You plan to trade with the British?"

Doggy splashed through the puddle heedlessly. "At the moment, there aren't many who can speak their language."

"And you can?" I asked.

"No," Doggy said, giving little hops as he shook drops first from one wet shoe and then the other, "but my uncle can a little. He's worked at the Thirteen Factories and has been getting to know people. He's saved up enough to start a company. He figures that the foreigners are more likely to deal with someone who knows their language and customs."

I stared at the boy in his plain cotton clothes and ragged shoes. "I hadn't realized you were so ambitious, Doggy."

Pinching his sleeve, he wagged the dark material. "Why do you think I don't wear fancier clothes? I'm going to need a fat purse for what I have planned."

"I always assumed you needed to pay off something like gambling debts," I confessed.

He looked hurt. "Is that all you think of me? I've got my plans, I have."

I felt relieved in a way that he wasn't some aimless loafer but had grand ambitions. "You can learn a lot about someone from his dreams. I misjudged you, and I'm sorry," I said contritely.

He nodded that my apology was accepted. "And what about you, Miss? What are your dreams, if you don't mind me being so bold as to ask? You might think about your own future, too. Master Sung is a kind man, but he's been brought low, and so has his family."

I saw that he was genuinely concerned, and his words echoed some of my own thoughts. Did I really want to spend the rest of my life depending upon Master Sung's charity? My own situation had been precarious enough when he had been powerful. Now that he was in disgrace, things were twice as fragile for me.

But no. I couldn't be selfish. At the moment I had to worry about repaying Master Sung. "Just one problem at a time, if you please," I said, trying to hide my own worries.

Even the decorations at the Temple of the Five Genies didn't lift my spirits, though. Priests and the devout were putting up banners and ornaments because of the upcoming birthday celebration. Thousands of years ago, when Canton was young, the Five Genies had come in on rams and promised that the city would prosper and never go hungry. Then they rose into the Heavens to govern the five directions of the compass—north, south, east, west, and the center. However, their rams had remained, transforming into eternal stone as a sign of the prophecy. Even now, they kept an eye on Canton, protecting the city from plague. If a siege ever came, the priests were bound to parade their statues through the streets to help ward off sickness.

The happy scene at the temple was a sharp contrast to the one in the small square outside the prison, where several wretched creatures stood tied to stones or iron bars. Public humiliation was part of their punishment, and they stared at us with hopeless eyes as we passed.

The prison was next to the magistrate's offices,

where cases were judged and the daily tasks of the empire performed. However, the soldiers here were more intent on gambling than on guarding anything.

"You'd think there wasn't a war on," I muttered. Perhaps they thought as Master Sung did: that the British were too busy in India to attack us.

"Now would be a good time to start treating some folks to tea, Miss," Doggy murmured to me.

I blinked. "But we don't know them."

Doggy rolled his eyes. "You may know a lot about the world, Miss, but you don't know much on how it works. 'Tea money' is a polite phrase for a bribe."

What Doggy had said was true: I could rhyme a couplet or bargain with the butcher, but I realized that life in the Rats' Nest, though hard, was fairly straight-forward. Life within the city walls was far harder and more devious than life outside.

I swallowed. "I didn't bring any cash."

Doggy looked at me in amazement. "And Mistress didn't give you any cash when you left?"

"She must have forgotten," I said.

Doggy sighed and dug some coins from his sleeve.

"I expect to be repaid by someone."

"Don't worry," I said. "I'll talk to the mistress."

"Leave this to me, Miss." He wriggled his shoulders as if trying to relax. Then he swaggered up to a soldier, all smiles and breezy manner. If I hadn't known to watch, I would have missed the coins being passed from his palm to the soldier's.

Following the soldier's directions, we entered the magistrate's office and went down a corridor to a paper-filled room where a clerk sat fanning himself and sipping tea. He would have looked more at home at a picnic than in a wartime office.

Doggy passed him a few more coins and asked to see Master Sung.

The clerk set his fan down long enough to sweep the coins away. "All such requests must now be referred through the viceroy's new assistant, Lord Chin."

"He's risen high quite fast," I said bitterly.

The clerk smiled sourly. I don't think he lost any love on newcomers. "The viceroy knows who's his friend and who isn't. You'll find Lord Chin in his office."

His directions led us into the next building. It took

a couple of tries to find the office of the newly installed Lord Chin.

Here, at least, a clerk was busy scribbling on a sheet of paper. "We'll have the proclamation drafted for the viceroy in a little bit," he snapped without looking up. "These things take time."

It was difficult to read upside down, but I saw it was a proclamation to the British, telling them to leave. The viceroy seemed to think he could paper them to death.

"We didn't come for a proclamation," I said. "They said Lord Chin—"

He glanced up, annoyed, and then wiggled his fingers to shoo us away. "This isn't a nursery for children. Lord Chin is very busy with the war."

"We've actually come to see Master Sung," I explained. "He was arrested just last night."

The clerk sat back in his chair in surprise. "And what is the purpose?"

"He was taken away in his night clothes," I said and pointed to the bundle in Doggy's arms. "I've brought him some proper clothing."

"Denied," he said, and bent over the paper again.

"He has a right to clothes," I protested. "But perhaps you'll feel better after you've had some tea." I glanced at Doggy.

With a sigh, he slipped his free hand into his sleeve.

However, the clerk shook his head. "Only Lord Chin may sign the permission slip, and Lord Chin is too busy," the clerk said. Dipping his brush into the inkwell, he began to write again. "As am I."

The officious little man had tried my patience. "You've misspelled a word," I snapped.

"What? Where?" Annoyed, his eyes darted up and down the columns of words.

Even though Doggy was shaking his head not to irritate the clerk even more, I couldn't resist. "Here," I said, jabbing my finger against a word. "You're missing a stroke."

The clerk peered at the sheet. "That could have been embarrassing." He added the missing stroke.

"So you'll let us in?" I asked.

He smiled. "Denied." That must have been his favorite word.

Suddenly the door opened, and Lord Chin poked his head into the room. "I need someone to hang up a painting," he said.

"Doggy can," I said, and nodded to him.

Lord Chin stared at me in confusion for a moment, until he placed me. "Oh, yes, the orphan. Have you decided to haunt me, like a ghost?"

"I've brought clothes to my benefactor," I said. "Will you give me a permission slip to see him?"

Lord Chin shook his head. "I'm afraid that wouldn't be wise."

"It would only be common decency," I argued.

"But not very efficient, I'm afraid," Lord Chin said, "if we want him to sign a confession."

"A confession of what?" I demanded. I didn't add that his only crime had been to trust Lord Chin.

"My, aren't you the inquisitive little thing?" Lord Chin observed. "Well, you may add this little bit of trivia to your hoard of knowledge. Humiliation is part of the interrogation technique."

I felt Doggy's breath tickle my ear as he whispered, "He means Master Sung's being tortured."

I sucked in my breath sharply and stared up at Lord Chin, who merely spread his hands sadly. "Alas, the world is not as neat and tidy as a painting or a tapestry."

I should have given up right then, but I thought of Master Sung's kindnesses. "Isn't there anything that can change your mind?" Unfortunately, I didn't think a few of Doggy's copper coins would be enough to buy "tea" for Lord Chin's expensive tastes.

Suddenly he leaned his head to the side. "This is exquisite. Simply exquisite." I started as he leaned forward. Doggy balled his hands into fists, but I motioned him to stay put when I realized that Lord Chin was examining my jacket and trousers. "The stitchery is amazing. Is that your mother's handiwork?"

"Yes," I said, "it's the last thing she made."

"Now, there's provenance!" he said, smacking his palms together.

If I had disliked him before, I hated him now for being so ghoulish, but I hid it well. "Might I see your collection of my parents' work sometime, Lord Chin?" Sometimes the value of a collection isn't in the collection itself but in being able to show it to someone.

"Yes, you of all people should be able to appreciate it," he said. "Come." He led us into an office with a huge teak desk. Books stood in stacks around the walls, waiting for bookcases.

Draped over them were several of my father's landscapes, which had been attached to expensive silk backgrounds. Next to them were the embroidered copies that my mother had sewn.

I have to confess that I forgot my errand for a moment. I started to reach my hand out to touch one, but stopped myself in time. "I remember when Father painted this waterfall. It was pouring rain outside."

"Indeed?" Lord Chin said, studying the painting and then wiggling his fingers at it. "Yes, that's why he caught the flowing quality of the water." He pointed to the embroidered version, where the waterfall shimmered in blue and green and white silk. "And when did your mother make this?"

I massaged my forehead as I tried to remember. "It was much later. I think it was a hot day."

"Yes, yes," Lord Chin nodded eagerly. "That's why

the water is so tantalizing."

One by one, we went through the other paintings and embroidery. It was like walking through my memories as I recalled happier times with my mother and father.

As I reminisced, Lord Chin became more and more pleased. "You're a regular treasure trove, my dear. Your stories will make my pieces all the more valuable."

"Truly?" I asked in amazement. "When Father sold something, he barely made enough to cover his paints and my mother's silk thread."

"It's tragic they died when they did. People were just starting to appreciate their work." He heaved a sigh. "You must visit me again, when I have time, and tell me more. But at the moment, I must attend to business. There's so much to do if we are going to save the city."

I felt as if someone had splashed cold water on my spine. I wondered if that "business" included torment-ing Master Sung more.

I stroked my sleeve for a moment. It was my last reminder of my parents. What would they have wanted me to do? Suddenly, I knew what I had to do. They would have told me to help their friend.

"You have such a fine collection, but wouldn't this be the prize?" I asked, pointing to my jacket.

"You can't," Doggy blurted out.

Lord Chin hesitated. "Your mother's last work?"

"It would make you the envy of every other collector," I coaxed.

"I suppose Sung will crack anyway," he said thoughtfully, but then he shook his head. "It's tempting, but I'd better refuse."

I held out the hem of one sleeve. "But it's some of her best work."

"Indeed," he nodded regretfully, "but even I have limits to my greed. Believe me, child, when I say you do not want to see Master Sung at the moment."

"I would see my father's friend anytime," I insisted, "and at any price."

Lord Chin studied me sadly. "Such loyalty is rare nowadays." Perhaps I had even shamed him a little for his own betrayal. But then he shook it off. "If everyone gave the same loyalty to the emperor, the empire would have nothing to fear. Well, you shall have your wish, but you've been warned about what you will see." And Lord Chin called to his clerk to bring him a permission slip—and some old clothes for me.

10 *Hope*

I gave a little gasp when I saw Master Sung huddled in the tiny cell. Bruises covered his face, and I assumed from the way he sat and leaned forward on an old mildewed mat that there were more bruises all over his body. The smell of urine and unwashed bodies filled my nose.

Master Sung uncurled from the mat like an old dog. His first thought was of me. "What are you doing here?" he asked in amazement.

I wanted to cry, but I thought tears might make him feel worse, so I did my best to hold them back. "We've brought you some decent clothes," I said, motioning to Doggy.

"This is no place for a young lady," he said, shaking his head. When he raised a hand to wave me away, it shook terribly.

"Begging your pardon, sir, but I don't think anyone else could have talked her way in," Doggy said, setting down his bundle.

Master Sung's puffed and bleeding lips stretched in a small smile. "I don't doubt that." Then he peered at me closer. "But what are you doing in those rags? We should have better clothes made for you."

I was now wearing an old, holey blue blouse and black slacks. The sleeves and trousers were so long that I'd had to roll them up. And from the bites I felt, I was sure that I was sharing these clothes with fleas. "There's no need. I have better things at home." Master Sung had enough on his mind without worrying about my sacrifice, too.

Doggy, though, was never shy. "She gave up the outfit her mother made for her. That Lord Chin took a fancy to the stitching."

"Oh, child." Master Sung tried to sit back, but winced.

"What have they done to you?" I started to rush toward him, but the folds of my pants fell and I almost tripped.

Leaning on one elbow, he stretched out a hand to catch me. "They are trying to persuade me to confess."

"But you have a right to protest against useless taxes," I insisted.

His supporting hand had started to tremble, so he dropped to the floor. "Unfortunately, the viceroy does not see it that way," Master Sung said, "and I suspect Lord Chin is maneuvering to confiscate our property."

"That's what Mistress Sung thought," I said. And then I whispered in his ear, "She's doing what she can to protect it."

"Thank Heaven," Master Sung said. We all jumped when we heard the distant screams. "Poor Ma," Master Sung said, shaking his head. "It's his turn right now; but they're beginning to use even more forceful methods of persuasion."

I began to roll up my trousers, but that motion made my sleeves slip down again as well. "We have to get you out before they start on you again. It might take a lot of 'tea,' but we will."

"No," he said forcefully. "Tell Mistress Sung that she

is not to bankrupt the family."

I shivered as the screaming went on. "But when I tell her what's going on—"

"You mustn't," Master Sung ordered. "You must tell her . . ." When he tried to lick his injured lips, he winced again, ". . . that I am well."

"But—" I began to protest.

Master Sung straightened proudly. "River Rats aren't the only ones made of stern stuff."

"I can see that," I said respectfully, then promised, "I'll find a way to see you again."

"No," Master Sung commanded me again. "Soon I won't be fit for anyone's eyes."

One can find bravery in the most unexpected places. "Rats aren't squeamish," I said.

Doggy cleared his throat. "If you leave it to me, sir, I bet I can smuggle packages in to you. It's just a question of treating the right jailer to tea."

It was becoming an effort for Master Sung to keep his head up, and he lowered it wearily as he spoke to me. "There. Will Doggy's plan satisfy you?"

"But that doesn't seem like enough," I said.

"If you want to do something for me," Master Sung said, sinking back onto the mat, "help my wife."

"I already am," I said. "And I'll keep on as long as she'll let me."

He stretched out a hand to pat me clumsily on the arm. "You're like another daughter."

I wasn't sure I wanted to be a sister to the pampered little pets in his mansion, but I said politely, "Thank you. You've been as kind as any father."

The screaming began again as we left the cell. I forced myself to keep walking. "If the food is anything like the accommodations, he'll starve to death," I said to Doggy.

"Leave it to me," Doggy vowed. "I'll get decent food to him. As my granny says, 'There's never a jailer who isn't thirsty for some tea.'"

When we returned to the mansion, Wing, the gatekeeper, told me that the family wanted to see me immediately. However, I could hardly go in my present clothes. "In a moment," I said.

I went hastily to my room to change. It was there that Miss Emerald tracked me down.

"Mother wants to see you right away," she said.

The borrowed blouse was over my head at the moment, so I was blind. "I just wanted to freshen up."

"What are you doing dressed as a peasant?" she demanded.

Hastily I pulled off the blouse. "I . . . I didn't want to get dirty."

Miss Emerald held her nose. "You've never been so fastidious when you've been rooting around in the garden dirt."

I tried to shift subjects. "I know you're anxious to hear . . . your father is well." I felt bad, lying like that, but that was Master Sung's command. I tried to ease my mind by tossing in a bit of the truth. "And he was thinking of you. He doesn't want you to worry."

Miss Emerald lingered while I finished changing. "Did he say when he was coming home?"

"I'm afraid not," I said. I tried not to think of the torture, because the horror might show in my face.

Still Miss Emerald stayed. "I . . . I would have gone if I'd been asked, but my parents treat me like I'm porcelain. But I'm not delicate at all."

I could hear the hurt in her voice, but I couldn't help wondering what would have happened if she'd seen her father. Would she have fallen apart, or was she as tough as her father and mother?

I tried to spare her feelings, though. "Of course, you aren't," I assured her, "but your family needed you more. No one needs me."

"Thank you, at least, for saying that," she said and slipped from the room.

After a quick brushing of my hair, I went to Mistress Sung's bedroom, where the rest of the family waited for us. It was easier to tell the lies a second time, and it would probably be even easier the next.

I felt guilty when Blessing, Miss Willow, and Miss Oriole looked relieved. "I think we can manage to get parcels in to him," I added, "so he can feel more comfortable."

"We should send him his favorite book of poetry," Blessing suggested. I hadn't realized he could be so thoughtful.

"And we should all write him a letter," Miss Willow suggested.

"I'll draw him a picture," Miss Oriole said.

I thought to myself that I would also make sure there were some salves for his bruises and cuts. Those would be just as wanted as books and letters. As I saw the relaxed faces, I began to think Master Sung was right to protect his family from the truth.

Miss Oriole was full of plans for the package. If the situation had not been so dangerous, it would have been amusing to see what she considered essentials for living. Frankly, I was not sure Master Sung could even hold a fan in his hand—even if the handle was made of ivory.

Miss Willow teased her. "If it was up to you, the package would fill a cart."

"We have to smuggle it in, you fool," Blessing said.

"Who's the fool?" Miss Oriole demanded and gave him a playful shove. The scene was almost normal.

Mistress Sung clapped her hands sharply together. "You can take your play outside," she said. As I started to follow them, she called to me, "Spring Pearl, will you stay? I have something else to discuss with you."

There was something in her voice that gave me a

bad feeling, but I said, "Yes, Mistress."

As the others left, Miss Emerald shut the door behind them, staying in the room.

"Emerald, go watch Blessing, and make sure he doesn't torment his sisters too much," Mistress Sung commanded.

"If anything, he's the one in danger," Miss Emerald said. "I'd rather be here when you talk to Miss Weed."

"It isn't necessary," Mistress Sung said.

Miss Emerald stamped her foot. "Mother, I know something is wrong."

I glanced at her and wondered again how tough she actually was. Mistress Sung was having the same doubts. "I don't think you really want to hear."

There was something different about Miss Emerald, though. Maybe it was her back that was a little straighter. Or perhaps it was because there was less of a pout to her lips. I said, "Mistress, if you keep a bird in a cage, it never learns how to fly."

Mistress Sung hesitated, and then sighed, "Yes, I suppose so." Then she looked at me. "Now tell me what you *really* saw."

I shifted my feet uneasily. "I've already told you, Mistress."

"My husband," Mistress Sung said, "has always done his best to protect us from the ugliness of the world. So I know what he would want you to tell me."

"But he ordered me, Mistress," I begged.

"And I am ordering you to ignore him," Mistress Sung said. "I have to have the truth if we are to save him and the family."

"He was concerned about your future . . . " I said. "Maybe that's more important than my promise to him." So I told them about the cell and the torture. With each detail, their faces grew more and more horrified.

"We must win Father's release," Miss Emerald said.

"But not at the cost of bankrupting the family," I said. "He was very clear about that."

Mistress Sung's chin had sunk to her chest. She raised her head now as if it weighed a hundred kilos.

"And he's right," she said. "The family comes first."

"Mother, we can't abandon him," Miss Emerald protested.

"We aren't," Mistress Sung said. "I swore we'd wait for him, and we will. And until we free him, we'll try to make him comfortable in his cell—if we can." She glanced at me. "But right now we should hide the deeds and goods."

I thought of Master Sung's determination. It would take more than a little torture to make him confess. "He's not going to give them any excuse to confiscate his family's property. He has more of a warrior's heart than a lot of these military peacocks strutting about through the streets."

Mistress Sung lifted her head proudly. "Of course."

"I want to help," Miss Emerald said. "Teach me, please," she begged and then looked at me. "Both of you."

I had wronged her by thinking that her mind was filled just with fluff. There was some of her parents in her, after all.

Miss Emerald did not know a lot, but she proved herself a good student, helping Mistress Sung and me, as well as Blessing. She also didn't feel the snubs as keenly as Miss Willow did, now that all their wealthy

friends were avoiding them because their father was
in prison.

And Miss Emerald really proved her worth when
she kept Blessing from enlisting in the army.

"But if I join, we'll prove our loyalty," he argued.

"Courage won't be enough against British guns,"
I pointed out.

Miss Emerald, though, knew how to handle her
brother. "And if something happens to you while
Father's in prison, the family loses everything." She
put a hand on his arm. "We know you're brave. You
don't have to prove it to anybody."

I picked up on my cue quickly. "You'll have plenty
of chances when the British come."

"So you say," Blessing shrugged. "But I should've
been the one to go to Father."

I tried to soothe his hurt feelings. "You were doing
what you needed to do—which was protect the family."

However, it didn't sit any better with him than it
had with Miss Emerald that I'd been the one to go
to their father. "I'll show everybody that I'm just as
capable as Miss Weed."

I have to say that he stuck with it—to the surprise of his mother and sisters. And it was good that he did, for those were busy times for all of us.

The Sungs' affairs included business in all parts of the city. Mistress Sung, Blessing, and I had to journey about just as Master Sung once had. But no matter where we went, we made sure that our trips included two extra stops.

The first was the prison. Fortunately, it had taken Doggy only a few days to develop a channel to Master Sung. Mistress Sung not only repaid him what he had advanced, but she gave him a generous allowance for future bribes. Soon food and medicines were flowing to Master Sung. How much that would help, we didn't know. We could only hope.

The other stop was at the city walls by the river to see how the war was going. At the beginning of winter, the British had returned with even more ships and troops, and French ships had steamed up the river beside them. Oddly enough, though, this time our troops had done almost nothing to stop them. They had not sent the floating torpedoes again and had fired only a couple of shots at them from the cannon.

Standing on top of the wall, we saw the enemies' steamships floating on the river, as sleek and deadly as wolfhounds. Tubby little gunboats were moored alongside them. I couldn't help glancing toward my old home. The shacks by the riverbank were deserted. Rats were good at escaping—just as we did whenever the river flooded and sent us scrambling from our homes.

The only things that Viceroy Yeh bombarded the British and French with were letters and proclamations ordering them to leave. It was almost as if he thought he could will them away. However, he had executed more than four hundred Chinese rebels and hung their heads on the wall as a warning to the foreigners of what would happen to them. Mistress Sung thought that the viceroy had become a mad beast, and I was inclined to agree. I had started to worry that Master Sung would become his next victim. Sometimes, when she thought no one was looking, Mistress Sung bit her lip as if that concerned her, too.

So we were surprised when we saw them dismantling

the defenses at the gate. "What are you doing?" Blessing asked one of the guards.

He shrugged. "It's the viceroy's orders."

I was astounded. "So the British and French gave in?"

"Not that I know of," the guard said, "but the viceroy must have worked out some sort of deal. We're probably paying them off." He looked disgusted.

For the first time in over two months, I began to hope.

"If the war is ending," I said to Mistress Sung and Blessing, "maybe they'll release Master Sung."

"I hope it'll be soon," Mistress Sung nodded. When she turned, she saw a street stall below. "Persimmons," she said. "I haven't had one in years."

"Then let's have some," Blessing suggested, "in celebration."

Doggy's granny, though, could have warned us not to build our mansion before we had the money in our hand.

11 Roots

At first I thought it was a thunderstorm, and I sat up groggily. Then I heard the distant explosions and felt the ground shaking faintly.

The floor was cold, and I shivered as I pulled on my shoes and padded outside. The maids were panicking, as usual. Miss Oriole was already in her doorway.

She held out a hand to me. "Miss Weed, what's happening?"

"I don't know, but I'm going to find out," I said, and then raised my voice so the maids could hear. "Stop it!"

I had to repeat myself several times, with Miss Oriole adding her voice to mine. By then, Miss Emerald and Miss Willow had come into the hallway. Miss Willow stood there blinking sleepily, but Miss Emerald helped me calm everyone down.

"I'm going outside to see what's happening," I announced to all of them.

Miss Emerald gripped my arm tightly. "Be careful."

"I will," I promised.

I was back in my room, changing into my good jacket and trousers, when my jail rags caught my eye. Those might be more suitable for a scout, so I slipped them on instead. Then I braided my hair into a man's queue. In the loose blouse and with a hat, I would pass for a boy. Girls were always doing that in *kung-fu* novels.

The maids were huddled quietly in one spot in the hallway under the watchful eye of Miss Emerald.

"Really," Miss Willow said in distress when she saw me, "you can't leave the house looking like that!"

"No one will notice her in that outfit," Miss Emerald

said. She was catching on fast.

Mistress Sung herself was down in the front courtyard, listening to the explosions. There was a faint smell of gunpowder in the winter air. "The British and French ships are bombarding the city," she said.

I turned to see where she was pointing and saw the smoke rising from the river and spreading across the sky in an evil dark cloud. I hoped my fellow Rats were all right.

"I'll try to find out what's going on," I said as I turned to leave.

Mistress Sung shook her head. "It's too dangerous."

"I've dodged bullies and muggers all my life," I boasted. "The British and the French are nothing." I tried to sound more confident than I felt. "Mistress, we have to know what's going on. And in the meantime, you might want to take everyone down to rooms where shells can't get them."

Mistress Sung hesitated, and then she brushed a hand over her forehead. "Yes, you're right. But don't go too far."

She turned, beginning to give orders in a clear, firm

voice. Our defenders could have used her on the walls. Grabbing a servant, I borrowed his hat.

Doggy himself was waiting by the gates. "I thought you might be poking your nose outside."

"Curiosity is my biggest sin," I admitted.

"The only trouble is that there're a lot of folks with worse sins who'd do something nasty to you." He scratched his cheek. "So I guess I'd better tag along again to keep you out of trouble."

"There won't be any profit in it for you," I teased, but I was glad of the company.

"Don't worry about me," Doggy grinned. "As my granny says, 'Even the worst flood always leaves some treasures behind.' I'll keep an eye on the street. There's always a few lost bits of cash to find, and I bet money will be just spilling out with everyone rushing around."

However, the streets were deserted as we made our way to the city walls. As we walked, I felt a lump that was beginning to make my left foot ache. "These shoes must be a pair that I made," I sighed.

The thundering grew louder as we neared the gates, until I felt like I was sticking my head into the middle of a storm. When we rounded the last corner near the gates, we were just in time to see the disaster.

We saw a pack of our troops break from the tower, but this was no orderly march. Spears and swords clanged against the stones as they threw them away as they ran.

An officer roared at them, "Stand fast!"

I don't think they even heard him. Their eyes were wide with terror, and the only thing that seemed to be on their minds was to get away. "The foreign soldiers are landing!" one of them cried.

"The panic's spreading," Doggy whispered to me.

The street beneath the wall was filled with troops. I blinked, unable to believe it was happening. They had been swaggering about the city for months, bragging about how they were going to chase the British away this time.

Another unit of soldiers fled past us. "We can get out by the North Gate," one man panted to another.

Even the uniformed soldiers were joining the rout, and there were now huge gaps on the parapet where China's defenders had fled.

The troops couldn't wait to escape to their homes. I could hold my own against bargain hunters when Uncle Soo was holding a sale on pork, but this was like being caught in a stampede of water buffalo. I was glad Doggy was with me.

The fleeing troops swept us through the city as if we were pieces of driftwood. Several times I tripped and almost went down. I was sure I would be trampled, but each time Doggy's strong hand grabbed my arm and hauled me back to my feet.

The really hard part came when it was time for us to leave the human river. Getting out of the crush of people was like fighting against a strong current full of rocks and tree branches. Doggy and I both used our elbows, and I even saw him butt heads a few times. But we finally broke free into one of the cross streets not far from the Sung mansion.

Then we just stood there gasping for a moment. I'd lost my hat and my hair tumbled loose down my back. His shirt was torn, he'd lost a shoe, and his eye was bruised.

"You're hurt," I said, raising a hand. "Your eye's

going to be really black-and-blue tomorrow."

Doggy took his wound in stride, though. "I'm glad it hurts. Only a corpse feels no pain."

We saw more people trying to flee, and not just soldiers. Some of them had baskets on poles—which I doubted would last long amid all the bumping. Others seemed to have thrown what they could into quilts they had bundled on their backs. Children cried as their parents dragged them along. One man was so busy saving his prize fighting rooster that he almost forgot to hang onto his son's hand.

As we threaded our way through the crowd, I could feel my stomach tightening with fear. It was a relief to finally see the walls of the Sung mansion, but we also saw the gates of their neighbors open. Through the gateway, half-dressed servants carrying a dozen sedan chairs lurched toward us like a flock of drunken birds. Behind them staggered servants carrying chests and boxes.

We barely got out of the way in time, hugging the walls as we moved toward the Sungs' gates. "We'll be doing that soon ourselves," Doggy said. "Let's see if that old turtle of a gatekeeper has run off." And he began thumping his fist against the heavy door and yelling.

Wing had stayed at his post. We heard the crossbar sliding off the holders, and then one of the gates swung back.

"What's happening?" Wing asked anxiously.

"We've lost," I said, and pushed past him. "The army's deserting the wall."

Servants converged on us and began to ask the same question as Wing. "I must see Mistress Sung. Where is she?" I demanded.

"In the mansion somewhere," Cook said, waving his hand.

I left Doggy to deal with their questions while I headed inside. More servants and maids tried to stop me, but I told them I would be with them shortly. Right now, I had to see Mistress Sung.

Someone said she was in her room. Another said she was in the master's study. I wasted precious time looking for her.

Finally Miss Emerald found me. "Miss Weed!" she

said. "We were starting to worry about you. What happened?"

"Our bold warriors have deserted us," I said bitterly. "Where is Mistress Sung?"

"Mother's in the garden," Miss Emerald said, then hesitated. "I think all the catastrophes have made her lose her wits."

"Mistress Sung?" I asked in surprise. She was the most levelheaded person I knew, and Miss Emerald's words shook me. "What is she doing there?"

"See for yourself," Miss Emerald said, taking my hand.

She led me down into the garden where her sisters and brother were standing, staring at their mother as she sat on a drum-shaped porcelain stool under a flowering quince tree that was next to some jasmine.

I had been expecting to see some wild-haired, raving madwoman, but she was dressed in one of her best robes and her hair was as neatly coifed as ever. It was only when I got closer that I saw she had taken off her shoes and was running her bare feet back and forth in the dirt.

It was such a change from her usually elegant appearance that I hesitated.

"Pearl!" she said with a relieved smile and held out her hands.

"M-Mistress Sung," I said uncertainly.

As Miss Emerald let go of my hand, she gave me a nudge. "Humor her."

I stepped forward and clasped her fingers. "Are you all right?"

"I'm fine, now that you're back safe. What's the news?" she demanded.

"It's all bad," I said, hearing the gasps behind me. Quickly I filled her in on what had happened. "The foreigners will invade the city soon. But we can still escape through the North Gate."

"I've promised my husband that we would be here waiting for him." Mistress Sung went back to shuffling her feet in the earth. "And I intend to keep that oath."

"But Master Sung wouldn't want you to take that kind of risk," I protested.

"It will be as dangerous outside the walls as within," Mistress reasoned. "So don't worry about us, Pearl.

We'll be safe inside our locked gates. Now, go change and have some breakfast."

That hardly sounded like a madwoman. Just being near her, I felt a calm courage, too. "Yes, Mistress," I said and motioned to the shoes by her feet. "Would you like me to bring water for you to wash your feet before you put those back on?"

Mistress Sung wriggled her toes in the dirt. "When I was a girl on our farm, I used to love feeling the earth on my bare feet. I loved the smell of green, growing things. When I came here, I was so busy trying to be the rich matron that I ignored the plants here." She stretched a hand up to draw a branch of quince down, and sniffed it. "How silly I was. You've done well, Pearl." Smiling at me, she shoved her feet deeper into the soil. "Even rich families have to have roots. Now, children, everybody . . . off with your shoes!"

Her children looked embarrassed as they took off their shoes, but I was glad to dig my toes into the dirt.

"You must keep on bringing back the garden, Pearl," Mistress Sung commanded. "Oh, but look at your hair! It's such a fright. Lean forward a little, dear."

And she began to undo what was left of my braid. "Blessing, pick some jasmine, like a good boy."

I tilted my head forward a bit as she used her fingers like a comb to untangle my hair. The rhythmic sweep of her arm was powerfully soothing, and she began to hum pleasurably to herself—just as my mother had when she had brushed my hair.

When a puzzled, barefoot Blessing brought over a spray of the delicate flowers, Mistress Sung began to entwine it in my hair. "Pick more for your sisters, will you, Blessing? I used to do this all the time when I was their age. It's so much prettier than any jewelry."

As the sun warmed my face and the cool, moist earth embraced my feet, I felt like I'd become a flower myself.

12 The Return

I peeked through the gates, watching the street go crazy. The mansions poured out hordes of people fleeing the invaders. Servants, carrying their masters and mistresses in sedan chairs, struggled to make headway through the other refugees. Chests of money and jewelry flowed out of the houses on the backs of the servants. To be honest, I think I would have left the antique dressers and vases in the mansions, no matter how valuable they were.

And the noise! There were babies and children bawling their heads off. People were shouting for lost relatives or cursing at anyone who got in their way. It reminded me of a time when a herd of pigs got loose in the Rats' Nest.

Then suddenly the street was deserted. I felt like a

ghost as I stared out at the now-empty mansions. The British and French, though, did not assault the walls that day. Instead, they kept firing their guns in a slow, steady rhythm. Some of their shells flew in high arcs and landed deep in the city.

At night, the sky glowed red from the fires and from the sparkling trails of the rockets the foreigners had begun to shoot off. I don't think anyone slept that night because of the booming of the guns and the smell of the smoke.

When the bombardment stopped the next morning, it was a shock. I wanted to go see what was happening, but Mistress Sung refused this time. "The guns probably stopped so their troops could assault."

After all the desertions, we now had too few men to

defend the entire wall. And those who were left chose
to defend the wrong part. The French climbed up
where no one expected them, and then the British
clambered up at another undefended spot. Once they
were on the walls, they drove the defenders away. By
that afternoon, the foreigners held the city walls.

And then they sat there, looking down at us over
their rifles. It was like being knocked down by a wolf
and then having the wolf just bare his teeth but not
bite your throat.

In the streets, watchmen went around reading aloud
an official proclamation from the Manchu general and
our provincial governor, Po. In it, they told everyone
to stay calm in this state of emergency.

However, after all his boasting about driving the
invaders away, the viceroy did nothing. Doggy and
the other servants brought back the rumors that were
flying around the city. Some thought the viceroy had
lost his senses. Others thought he was dabbling in evil
magic to drive the invaders away.

By the third day, I put on my ragged outfit and
slipped out the gates on my own to find out what I

could. A grumbling Doggy came along.

There were few people on the streets, but we caught glimpses of the blue uniforms of the foreign troops on the wall.

It was a shock to see armed foreign sailors in the goldsmiths' street. They were using their rifle butts to smash in the heavy doors.

Doggy pulled me back into a doorway, out of sight. "The invasion's starting. We'd better get back."

I risked another peek, though. "Right now they look more like thieves than warriors."

A sailor swaggered out of another store with gold chains draped around his neck and bracelets on his arm. I was sure his bulging pockets contained more treasure. When he said something to his friend, I didn't recognize the words, so I assumed they were French.

Doggy wanted to head back the way we came, but I shook my head. "I know these streets better than you. I can take us on a route where we won't see anyone."

"And what would you know about hiding?" Doggy demanded.

"Plenty," I said. "You've never tried to avoid gangs

who were out to steal your grocery money."

Grudgingly, he let me lead, and I took us down twisting alleys and narrow lanes covered by bamboo mats that hid the sun. I felt comfortable in this tunnel of shadows.

"You really are a Rat," he admitted.

However, I wasn't nearly as clever as I thought I was. Rounding a corner, I bumped right into a giant foreign sailor. His uniform was different from the uniforms worn by the looters we'd just seen. I would have fallen over, but he caught me with his free hand.

Doggy sprang to my defense. "Let her go," he said, raising a fist.

When the sailor next to my captor raised his rifle, I reached up and grabbed the barrel. "Stop," I said in English. "We don't mean you any harm."

The second sailor was so astonished that he lowered his gun. "You can talk."

Apparently he didn't consider Chinese real speech, but this didn't seem like the time to correct him.

"Of course I can," I said. "Quite well."

My captor let go of me. He had a sword and pistol

rather than a rifle, so I assumed that he was an officer. "You all right, girlie? I just grabbed you so you wouldn't fall."

"Yes, I'm fine," I said and then whispered to Doggy, "It's all right."

I didn't see their companion at first, because he was so short that the soldiers had hidden him. He was dressed in a frock coat and top hat.

"Spring Pearl?" he asked, peering at me.

"Mr. Fortescue!" I said in English.

Mr. Fortescue walked toward me with his hands out. "I was so hoping I'd find you. Are your father and mother well?"

"They passed away," I said. Even now, it hurt to have to say that.

He took my hands and gave them a squeeze. "I'm so sorry. Are you all right? Do you need help?"

"No, I'm well," I said. "I live with one of Father's friends, Master Sung."

"Indeed." Mr. Fortescue tipped his head back. "I've dealt with him and found him a fair man, but a hard bargainer. Is he treating you right? Can I help?"

I became aware of my ragged clothes. "These aren't my regular things," I explained hastily. "I only wore these when we came out to gather news. Master Sung's been very kind."

Mr. Fortescue glanced at the sailors and then spoke to me in Chinese. "Well, you can go back home and tell everyone not to worry. We should have peace soon."

"The viceroy is going to make peace?" I asked eagerly.

Mr. Fortescue shook his head. "No, but the provincial governor is working on terms privately. I've read the messages myself because I've been seconded to the military as an interpreter—thanks to your father's Chinese lessons."

"Then what are you doing here?" I asked. "We thought you were looters."

"We're on a scouting mission. They needed someone who could actually read the signs," Mr. Fortescue reassured me. "And despite the dangers, I've been rather enjoying my first jaunt *inside* Canton, after staring at the walls all these years. But you needn't worry. There are orders against looting."

"Well, some of the sailors are disobeying," I said and told him what we'd seen.

Mr. Fortescue frowned as he switched back to English. "They must have sneaked down into the city when their officers weren't watching."

"Foreign sailors must be as poorly paid as Chinese ones are," I sighed.

Mr. Fortescue squeezed my hands urgently. "Dear Pearl, it would be best if you go home right away. But when all this is over, you only need send word to me if you ever need anything."

"You'll be starting your business again, won't you?" I asked. If we were going to forge new bonds with the foreigners, we would need more like Mr. Fortescue.

He leaned away. "You could not keep me away from your lovely country. All this time, while I was in exile on the ships, I kept your father's landscape hanging near my berth."

"We should be going, sir," the sailor with the sword coughed politely.

"Yes, of course, Ensign, how thoughtless of me. I'm in the Navy now, aren't I?" Mr. Fortescue finally let go of my hands. "Be careful, and stay well, Pearl."

"You, too," I said.

Mr. Fortescue had to give a hop and a skip to catch up. As I watched him scurry away, Doggy said wonderingly, "You seem to be good friends with him."

"He's the kind of person it would be hard not to like," I said. "Business is just his excuse for living here."

"Do you know many other merchants?" Doggy asked.

"A few," I said. Doggy quizzed me about them, and I was surprised at how many I knew.

"So you know Americans, as well as British," he said, rubbing his chin.

"They all wanted to learn Chinese," I shrugged.

When we brought the news back to Mistress Sung, she ordered all the staff and family to arm ourselves so that we could mount sentry duty against looters. With her usual common sense, Mistress Sung had had chairs and cushions brought out to the front courtyard so the guards could be comfortable while on duty.

After changing my clothes, I went outside and found Mistress Sung and Doggy taking the first watch. "It's not your turn, Pearl," she said to me.

I settled into a chair next to her. "I might be able to convince foreign soldiers to go elsewhere."

"It's a small chance, but one worth taking," Mistress Sung agreed and resumed binding a slender knife to a broom handle with strong twine.

"Here," Doggy said and held out the hilt of a large kitchen knife. "I figured where there was trouble, you couldn't stay away." In his other hand, he had the cleaver that Cook used for cutting through bone.

"You have many talents, Mistress Sung," I said, laying the knife across my lap.

She kept her eyes on her task. "I come from the hills, where feuds are a way of life. All the villages have walls, and there were many times when my father went armed to his fields."

"Especially if you're a Hakka," I said.

"Yes, especially," she nodded. "Sometimes I think it was a mistake for us to keep to our ways and own tongue. We should have tried to fit in better."

"But that's what makes the Hakka what they are," I said.

"But 'the nail that sticks out gets hammered.' That's true of a people as well as of individuals." Mistress Sung glanced meaningfully at me as she finished the knot.

"What if you can't help but stick out?" I asked thoughtfully.

"You learn to fight." Rising, she stamped her right foot forward as she thrust at the air. Doggy and I watched open-mouthed as she stabbed and parried against an invisible foe. When she was done, she tested the bindings again. "Yes, that will hold."

"You're a master," I said in amazement. Things must have been very tough for her when she was a girl in the fields. It made her transformation into an elegant lady even more amazing.

"Hardly," she panted. "I know just one spear set, and I don't even do that very well."

"Does Master Sung know?" I asked.

"That's how we met," Mistress Sung chuckled, dabbing her sleeve at her damp forehead. "I nearly stabbed him. He had some business in our district, but night caught him on the road so he came to the village to ask for lodging. I thought he was a raider." She lost her smile as she thought of him. "I hope he'll be all right."

I thought of the determined man I had seen in the prison. "If you'll pardon me for saying so, Mistress, he would have made a good Rat. And it's a well-known fact that we Rats are hard to kill."

Mistress Sung smiled. "I know he'd take that as a compliment." Reassured, and to pass the time as we waited, Mistress Sung spoke of her younger days, when she'd had "the mud between her toes."

Though I was reluctant to leave, Mistress Sung made me go back inside with her later, assuring me that I would be the first to be summoned if looters came.

However, the looters did not come. We heard of incidents in other parts of the city, but the looters never reached our street. The worst complaint was that Mistress Sung ordered our food to be rationed as a precaution.

After seven days, the British and French lost patience with the slow pace of the negotiations and sent their troops into the city. The viceroy was taken as a prisoner to the foreign ships, and then the British placed Governor Po in charge. Though the commands came from his mouth, everyone knew it was the foreigners who put the words there.

Feelings ran high in the city. Some thought anyone who helped the foreigners was a traitor. Others, like Mistress Sung, thought the governor was just being practical. I had to agree with her. Until we had guns and ships as powerful as theirs, we would have to let them do what they wanted.

Governor Po, however, did do some things on his own. He arrested the treacherous Lord Chin, and others, for their crimes. And then he released some of the prisoners, like Master Sung and Mister Ma, whose only sin had been to ask for justice.

It nearly broke my heart to see Master Sung when

he stepped from the sedan chair. He looked very old and very frail—perhaps because the plumpness he had lost had been replaced by wrinkles. The clothes I had brought him were stained and torn. I wondered if the brown spots were his own blood.

However, he refused help, and tottered across the stones under his own power. "Home," he said, his face wreathed in a grin.

Mistress Sung bowed. "Welcome back."

Miss Oriole was less ceremonious. She ran to her father and nearly bowled him over.

For once, the older children forgot their dignity and ran to him, too. I felt sad as I watched Master Sung fuss over and pet his children. Neither my mother nor my father could ever do that for me. Watching that warm scene, I felt like the odd duck, so I turned away.

"Pearl. Where's Spring Pearl?" Master Sung called.

I pivoted with a lump in my throat. "You did well," he said, and gave me a smile but no hug.

I was, after all, "his orphan" and not family. "Thank you," I said politely. "I was only trying to repay some of your kindness."

"Come, come," Miss Oriole urged, tugging at her father's hand. "You've got to see the spear Mother made. She's going to teach me how to stick someone with it."

"So you can find a husband just like your mother did?" Affectionately, Master Sung patted his youngest daughter's head. "Just make sure your aim is as bad as hers."

"I've told you a thousand times. I chose a spot that wouldn't be lethal." Mistress Sung poked his ribs indignantly. "Anyway, you had no business blundering into our valley at night."

"You should have known I was no robber," Master Sung laughed, sounding like his old self. "What self-respecting thief would make as much noise as I did?"

"Or squeal," Mistress Sung chuckled. "My father thought I'd stuck one of our pigs by mistake."

"And he was relieved when it was me instead," Master Sung recalled.

"You weren't expected to provide the main dish at New Year's," Mistress Sung shrugged.

Miss Oriole, of course, insisted that she was never

going to marry one of those "awful" boys. As the Sungs began to tease one another, I felt even more like an intruder. Mistress Sung had done my hair that other day but, even so, I was still an outsider.

I gave them privacy by retreating to the garden. There, I did my best to help the plants that the soldiers hadn't trampled flat. I fussed over them as much as I wished my parents could still fuss over me.

13 *The Warriors*

Under his family's loving attention, Master Sung grew stronger every day. But I like to think that my garden also played a role. Mistress Sung brought him out to see the plum and cherry and quince trees, which had just begun to bloom. Under the pink and white canopy he would sit, a shawl wrapped around him against the cool air, and munch on the yellow-orange loquats that I picked for him while the sun and the scents washed away the horrors of the prison.

In the meantime, an uneasy peace settled on Canton. Things seemed to be going back to normal, but as I walked through the streets, I felt a tingling at the back of my neck. People were out and about again, but no one stopped to chat or gossip. They scuttled to do their errands and then hurried home. It was as if the city were holding its breath, waiting for something worse to happen.

Though I felt uneasy out in the city, I had taken it upon myself to help fatten up Master Sung by doing the shopping. Cook was pleased with my skills. I brought back far better groceries and at a cheaper price than anyone else did. Mother and Father had always left such things to me. When you don't have a lot of money to spend, you develop a knack for haggling. And even though I now had a fat purse, old habits die hard.

Only Doggy was unhappy with the new arrangement, because it was his misfortune to carry my purchases. "You take twice as long and buy twice as much," he complained.

"At a quarter of the price," I reminded him, giving a little skip. I was becoming used to his ways. He was never happy unless he had something to grumble about.

He twisted his head to say something but shut his mouth. His eyes were gazing past me. When I turned to stare in the same direction, I saw the little dots of blue on the walls—it was the uniforms of the foreign soldiers and sailors. It was impossible to forget who really ruled the city now.

The last item on my list was a bolt of red cotton, so Doggy and I turned into another street. It was lined with stores selling every type of cloth and in every color of the rainbow.

"This is going to take forever," Doggy groaned.

"Heaven help your uncle when you join his business," I teased. "You don't have the patience for bargaining."

"I can do well enough," he said, annoyed, "but my time is valuable. I don't have to squeeze every piece of cash."

"You've always had the Sungs to take care of you,"

I said stiffly. "My family had to take care of itself."

Doggy dipped his head apologetically. "I've been to your house. In some ways, I *was* better off."

I felt a bit embarrassed that a servant would pity a scholar's family. "The Sungs are kinder than most masters, aren't they?"

"That's the truth," he nodded. "They've always been that way, at least to me. They treated my grandfather and father just as well. That's why the other servants think I'm crazy for wanting to leave their service."

I glanced at him. "Freedom means that much to you?"

"You've seen the new generation," he grunted. "What do you think they'll be like when they take charge?"

It was true enough, but I felt I ought to defend them, even so. "They're coming around."

Doggy still looked skeptical, but before he could say anything, we saw a storekeeper pelt past us. In his arm, he had a small strongbox. "Run! Run! The devils are coming! They'll kill us!"

We had barely stepped out of the way when a crowd

of terrified clerks and shopkeepers followed at his heels. They carried strongboxes or bolts of rare silk that they did not want to leave behind.

In the wink of an eye, Doggy and I were standing alone among the abandoned shops. Hats and even shoes marked the trail of the fleeing merchants.

A moment later, a squad of foreign soldiers smartly rounded the corner.

Doggy dropped his bundles. "Maybe we'd better get out of here, too."

I began to pick them up and stuff them back into his arms. "Honestly!" I teased. "How are you going to do business with them if you run away every time you see them? They've been flogging looters. This is probably a patrol."

Doggy glanced at me nervously. "If our soldiers'd had your backbone, the foreigners would never have gotten inside."

"They're not monsters," I said.

However, as the column drew near us, I began to second-guess my words. The only two foreign warriors I had ever met had been with Mr. Fortescue. These soldiers were as tall as giants and as stern as statues. However, as they marched past us, a tall soldier with red whiskers and stripes on his sleeve winked at me.

Breathing a soft sigh of relief, I settled against a wall. "Do you think those clerks will return soon?"

"Here they come, slinking back already," Doggy said.

I saw some Chinese men turn into the other end of the street. Their arms were loaded with baskets. Two entered the first store, and I got ready to walk down to them when I heard a crash from within. More crashes followed from the next few stores as other men entered.

A moment later, a man emerged from one of the shops with his arms full of bolts of expensive silk. The man wore ragged cotton clothes, not expensive robes, so I knew he didn't belong there. "Let's go," I said. "They're looters!"

"They must be following the foreign soldiers," Doggy said. He was already waddling away.

"Give me some of that to carry," I said, snatching some of the bundles from his arms so we could make better progress.

The next street was as deserted as the last. I guess the foreign patrol had passed. Other streets were emptying fast, too, as we hurried along.

When we turned into Master Sung's street, the deserted mansions seemed like big, gloomy tombs. I gave a jump when I heard crashing from within one of them.

"Some of the looters aren't waiting for the barbarian patrols," Doggy said. "They're striking off on their own."

I began to take the rest of our purchases from his arms. "Go find the soldiers, and then use these words," I said, switching from Chinese to English. "'We need help.'"

It took Doggy a couple of tries to get the pronunciation right while I was taking on his load. "We need help," he repeated more or less in English, and then sped away.

As I staggered toward Master Sung's, I realized that Doggy'd had a right to complain. I really had loaded him down with quite a lot.

I kicked the unbarred gates open and dropped my parcels on the side to immediately alert the Sungs.

Master Sung was going to stay but he wanted to send the rest of us away to the interior of the house. "Don't think you can get rid of me that easily," Mistress Sung said with a smile.

To my surprise, their children didn't want to leave either. "This is our home," Blessing said. "We're going to defend it."

As the defenders gathered, though, I began to wish I hadn't sent Doggy off. We had armed ourselves with kitchen knives and broom handles to hold off the looters. Master Sung strode in front with the antique sword from his study. I just hoped it didn't fall apart on the first swing. All in all, it didn't seem like much to hold off an invasion. We could have used Doggy's strong arms.

By now, the crashes and thuds were growing closer. Mistress Sung gripped her homemade spear. "Our own kind are worse than the barbarians."

They didn't even bother trying to break through the gates, which we had barred again. They must have stood on one another's shoulders, because a head soon poked up over the wall itself. On the thief's head was an expensive cap that he must have stolen.

Master Sung raised his sword threateningly. "Enter at your own peril!" he shouted. He might have been more intimidating if he hadn't been shaking so badly that his sword looked like a reed waving in the wind.

The thief just laughed insolently, then hoisted himself so that he was straddling the wall. But the next moment, a jagged rock whizzed by my ear and hit the grinning thief. With a cry, he fell backward.

I turned to see that Mistress Sung had set her spear down and was picking up another piece of broken paving stone from the courtyard. "When I was a girl," she said, straightening, "it was my chore to keep the birds from the crops."

"You must have been deadly!" her son said.

"Get more ammunition," I said. While the rest of us hurried around to find more broken paving stones, Mistress Sung kept throwing. Her aim was accurate, but there were too many looters. A couple of them scuttled like spiders over the wall and dropped into the courtyard.

They were both wearing some of their loot. One robber had jewelry hanging around his neck and arms. The other was wearing an expensive brocade vest over his bare chest. Together, they began to throw off the wooden bar on the gates.

Perhaps inspired by his wife, Master Sung swung his sword at the thieves and shouted, "Forward." Then he charged.

My heart thumping, I followed. None of the servants came, but I was surprised to see all of the Sung children moving with me. In the end, good blood will always show.

We didn't have any skill with our improvised weapons, but fear and anger lent us energy. Unfortunately, Master Sung was as much a threat to us as the thieves. His sword cuts had more enthusiasm than accuracy, and we had to keep ducking.

However, because we were now by the gates, Mistress Sung had to stop throwing stones and more thieves began to drop around us.

The maids were hopelessly useless, standing there

shrieking in fear. Cook was just as frightened. However, Mistress Sung picked up her spear and charged forward to save her family.

We certainly needed her because we were now surrounded. Blessing and Miss Emerald had already been disarmed. Miss Oriole was squealing as a robber grabbed her—and then dropped her with a squeal to match hers when she bit him.

Miss Willow and I were standing back-to-back while Master Sung was flailing away with the sword. Though his blows kept missing, he had cleared a circle around himself. But he was tiring. He was puffing like a blacksmith's bellows and sweating more than he had probably ever sweated in his life. It was really only a matter of time before the looters captured him as well.

Suddenly, behind me, Miss Willow gave a yelp. I turned to see her in the arms of a thief in an expensive silk robe that flapped about his dirty legs. Raising my knife, I turned to stab him when he started to laugh.

I would have known that laugh anywhere. "Hammer?"

He twisted his head around to stare. "Pearl?"

"I didn't expect you to be here," I scolded. "What would Auntie say?"

"Don't tell her," he gulped. "She got sick when we had to leave our home. We needed money for medicine, but there aren't any jobs."

I knew his mother must be sick, because Hammer's queue was all tangled. If his mother had been well, she would never have allowed him to go out like that.

"Why didn't you come to me?" I asked, lowering my knife. "I would have helped."

"You know Ma," Hammer said. "She's a proud one."

"What would she think of your stealing?" I asked.

To Hammer's credit, he began to turn red. "It'd kill her if she knew."

Miss Willow wriggled free from Hammer's grasp. "You know this thief?"

"He's a fellow Rat," I said.

"So you'll be able to tell us where they hid the good stuff," another thief said, grinning at me. He had a scar down one cheek.

Hammer was feeling guilty, though. "Leave them alone. We've got plenty of other places to loot."

"You aren't going soft, are you?" the thief with the scar demanded.

Hammer was the last one with whom I would have picked a fight. Years of loading and unloading ships had given him plenty of muscles, and years of riverside brawls had taught him how to fight.

One moment the thief with the scar was upright and sneering, and the next he was flat on his back, choking.

"Who's soft?" Hammer asked with soft menace as he pressed his knee against the scarred thief's throat, ready to crush it.

The man's scar turned a strange lavender as the rest of his face turned purple, and then he slapped the cobblestones to indicate his surrender.

Hammer rose. "Anyone else want to cross me?" he challenged.

No one came forward, but someone else said in a grieved voice, "We can't go away empty-handed." He was rubbing his arm where Miss Oriole had bit him.

"Of course not," Master Sung said. "If you'll keep other thieves away, I'll pay you."

A thief in a gilded headdress suggested, "Why don't we just take it all?"

The scarred thief sat up. "Because it isn't worth it," he coughed and jerked his head at Hammer.

The thieves let the other Sung children go, and we all gathered around Master Sung protectively while he set a price with the thieves. It was a lot of money, but Master Sung didn't seem upset. I suppose it could have been worse.

When he had paid them, we unbarred the gates and the thieves trooped out. "Don't worry," Hammer promised me. "I'll stand guard myself."

"Do you trust him, Pearl?" Master Sung asked me.

"He's as honest as I am," I said. "He's just going through hard times."

Master Sung turned to Hammer. "When things settle down, call on me in the regular fashion—not over my wall. I'll find work for you."

Hammer blinked in disbelief for a moment, then bowed respectfully to Master Sung. "I can't thank you enough."

"I'll bring you some food and something to drink,"

I promised, "but it won't be as good as your mother makes."

"I beg your pardon," Cook said indignantly. "I might be of little use on a battlefield but I know what I'm doing in a kitchen. I'll make him a feast."

In the meantime, Mistress Sung had dropped her spear and stretched her arms as wide as she could so that she could try to hold her husband and her children all at the same time. "Don't ever do that again," she scolded them.

Miss Oriole was squeezing what Sungs she could, but then she turned her head. "You come too, Miss Weed."

"Yes, come," Mistress Sung urged. "You're one of us now."

Blessing and Miss Emerald twisted to look at me at the same time. They both jerked their heads and Miss Willow waved a hand. "What are you waiting for, Spring Pearl?" she called. "You're family, too."

I had taken several steps forward before Miss Willow's words had sunk in: *Family*.

I must have picked up some grit in my eyes during

the fight, because I could feel them tearing up as I got my hug in turn.

Poor Doggy was the only real casualty. He never did catch up with the British patrol and finally came back to help. Unfortunately, I hadn't warned Hammer, so Doggy had wound up with a black eye with such vivid purples and blues that even Father couldn't have captured all the colors.

14 *The Flower*

Over the next month, mixed patrols of foreign soldiers and Chinese police brought some order to the streets. And floggings kept the foreigners and the Chinese from looting.

However, as we drew close to the New Year, the city stayed tense because of Chinese patriots who refused to give up the fight against the foreigners. Fighting a war from the shadows, they would ambush any foreign sailor or soldier who strayed too far into the alleys. The British and the French would then retaliate by burning down the houses in the area where the murder had happened. Their revenge reached a height when ninety-six Chinese were executed for the murder of a cook from a French ship.

Despite that, the British and French were going to

lift the blockade, and things were already beginning to return to normal. So was Master Sung. With rest and care, he had healed up and resumed work.

I finally had enough free time to return to my garden and clean it up a bit before the New Year's celebration. Just before New Year's, the Kitchen God always went back to Heaven to report about the household. It was a cheerful time when you reminded him of the nice things the family had done that year. It was a chance to recall only good memories. Then you bribed the Kitchen God by smearing his mouth with honey. After you burned the Kitchen God's picture, you bought another one to hang up in the kitchen.

The Sungs, as they did everything, would send the Kitchen God off more grandly than my parents had

done. A little altar had been set up in the front courtyard where we would set fire to the picture. There was
straw to feed the divine horses of his chariot as well.
At the same time, servants would toss beans and peas
on the roof over the kitchen to make a sound like
horses' hooves. However, this year, because of trigger-
happy foreigners, there would be no firecrackers.

To my dismay, I found that weeds had sprung up all
around my plants, so I began to work at clearing them.

I was so busy working that I didn't recognize Doggy
at first. He was in a formal cotton house jacket with
his collar buttoned up, and clean pants. Even the
crown of his head was freshly shaved and his queue
newly braided. There were still faint streaks of purple
and blue around the eye that Hammer had decorated.

"How's your war wound?" I asked.

"Fine, no thanks to you," he grumbled, pointing at
his wound. "It still hurts."

"At least I stopped Hammer before he broke your
arm," I teased.

Doggy, though, didn't look very grateful. "The
Master and Mistress want to see you."

I stood up in my grubby gardening clothes. "I'd better change then."

"There's no time." He seized my wrist. "They want to see you immediately."

"I can't go like this. Look at my clothes, and my hair's all tangled." Alarmed, I brushed a strand from my face.

"They said right away," Doggy insisted sternly, dragging me from the garden.

As he started to pull me toward the main hall, I protested, "But the study's that way."

"They're in the main hall," he snapped in exasperation. "Will you shut up for once and just listen."

I jerked my hand free and stopped. "I know how to listen as well as the next person. In fact, I'm a very good listener. People have said I'm like a jar that you can just pour words into."

Doggy just tapped his foot. "And when could they get a word in edgewise?"

"Humph, very well. I won't say a word to you all day." Straightening my sleeve and brushing my clothes, I stomped toward the main hall.

Doggy slipped a little ahead of me, taking the steps two at a time to the porch where the carved columns rose to support the gilded roof beams.

Almost at once, I began to regret my vow, since I was curious why he was dressed so formally. But an oath is an oath.

I was even more curious when he opened the tall doors for me. Since when had he become a gentleman? As I stepped across the threshold, I made a note to myself never to make such a rash promise again.

I came to a halt, though, when I saw Master and Mistress Sung in their formal robes seated in heavy teak chairs. On either side were their children in smaller chairs, all of them in exquisite clothes—though Miss Oriole was wiggling restlessly.

Standing in ranks on my left and my right was the entire household staff. They were all dressed as neatly as Doggy, who slipped over next to old Wing.

Master Sung scowled fiercely. "How dare you come dressed like that? This is a formal occasion."

I looked down at my filthy clothes, and a tangled strand of hair fell into my eyes as well. "I . . . I was told to come right away . . . so here . . . I am."

"It's an insult," Mistress Sung said gravely.

I dropped to my knees and bowed. "I'm sorry. It won't happen again."

Master Sung pounded the arm of his chair. "No, it won't! We've had enough of that."

Suddenly my stomach tightened. They were going to let me go! I just couldn't understand what I had done wrong. I thought I had become part of their family. I should have known my Rat-like ways would annoy them once too often. I had finally worn out my welcome.

It was strange, though. I felt only a little frightened at the prospect of being on the streets again. After all, I had survived a war—and even the Sung household. I was sure I could manage anywhere.

What I felt was sad. In this short time, I had come to like each of them in his or her own way. I felt like I was losing a second family. And I would miss my new garden most of all.

However, it wasn't in me to beg. After touching my forehead against the floor, I straightened. "Thank you for all you've done. As soon as I pack my things, I'll leave."

"You'll do no such thing," Master Sung thundered, and then his frown changed suddenly into a grin.

"You'll wear *this* for the next formal occasion, my dear." With a smile, Mistress Sung motioned to Miss Oriole.

Squirming off her seat, she rose with a package in her hands. I'd never seen her look so serious as she walked over to me. With a little bow, she held the package out to me.

It was wrapped in a lovely piece of green satin. As I felt the luxurious cloth, I thought of the wonderful things my mother could have made out of this.

"Well, don't just kneel there all day. Open it," Master Sung ordered, wiggling as much as Miss Oriole had.

Setting down the package, I undid the ribbon. I saw the flash of pink silk with the green border. "It's my clothes," I gasped, lifting them out.

Miss Oriole was gleefully bouncing up and down on her heels. "Papa got the British to take it back."

"Along with other confiscations. Mister For-tes-cue was a big help." Master Sung laced his fingers over his stomach, satisfied. "Tonight it is our wish that you wear it at the banquet, where you will be the guest of honor."

"Me?" I asked dumbly.

Miss Emerald spoke from the side. "We have survived because of you, Miss Pearl." So it was "Miss Pearl" and not "Miss Weed" anymore.

And she bowed. All of them did. Even the Master and Mistress.

And then I couldn't see them through the blur of tears. "Excuse me." Getting up, I stumbled from the hall. Nearly tripping on the steps, I made my way somehow back to the garden.

I needed to sit and think and catch my breath. Then I looked around. Strange how the mansion no longer looked like a fort—or a prison.

Suddenly a splash of red caught my eye. The camellia was finally blooming, spreading out large red petals. It liked its new home as much as I did. Later this year, I would prune it a bit, and then I'd use the cuttings to create more. With the goosefoot as a border for the future camellias, this area would look lovely.

That's where Doggy found me. "I'm sorry I couldn't warn you, but they wanted to surprise you. And you're such a terrible liar. You could never have faked it."

It was true enough, so I just shrugged.

He dug his shoe into the dirt nervously. "At any rate, I've got a proposition for you. My uncle's finally ready to start his business; and I've got my stake, so I'm going to join him soon as a partner."

I don't know why anyone would miss such an annoying boy, but the news made me feel sad. I simply nodded my congratulations.

He glanced at me and then deepened the furrow with his shoe. "But I was talking with my uncle. We both figure the British and the French are going to force China to open up to even more trade. The trouble is that there aren't enough interpreters. Not many can get their tongue around that *gobble-gobble* speech of the foreigners like you can. What's more important is that you've got the pull with the foreign merchants, as well as with Master Sung. But you can also talk the right way to the government folks, because they're all scholars. And yet, you can also handle the workers that load and unload the ships."

I'd never thought about it that way, but it was true enough.

He cleared his throat. "So, how about joining us?" He held up a hand. "And to sweeten the deal, we'll make you a partner in a few years, too."

Clutching my clothes to my chest, I stared up at him in astonishment.

"Sure, the Sungs treat you right, but you'll always be their dependent," Doggy said, waving a hand toward the main hall. "With us, you'll be free."

I loved the Sungs, and I thought all of them loved me now. So I believed them when they said I was part of their family. But *freedom*. The word was as potent as tiger whiskey. It made me feel almost dizzy.

"So what do you think?" Doggy urged. "In the old way of things, there wouldn't be much place for a servant like me or a poor girl like you, but the world's changing now. You got the talents and the friends. You'll be in demand."

When I still stared at him, stunned, he went on nervously, "I know how much you like dirt. You can have a garden, too—even if we have to put it up on the roof." He waved a hand at the camellia. "I'll even carry that flower myself."

I just stared up at him, still confused. Doggy, though, misinterpreted my silence. "If I insulted you before, I'm sorry. Feel free to talk anytime you want. I release you from your vow."

I'd forgotten my oath until now. And then, with a shake of my head, I just smiled.

He spread out his arms in frustration. "I just made you an offer most people would leap at. Why don't you say something?"

However, I only continued to grin.

Irritated, he rubbed the back of his head so vigorously that his collar popped open. "If you aren't the most annoying girl!"

I watched him stamp away, fuming and muttering. Revenge can be so very sweet.

As I savored my triumph, my eyes fell on the camellia. Would it take to new soil in yet another home? In my heart, I knew it could. It could survive anything—just like me.

Right then, a breeze brushed my ears, but it was almost as if my father and mother were whispering to me that I was going to be just fine. And stretching out my arms again, I turned my face once more to the sun.

The End

Then and Now ♦ *A Girl's Life*

C H I N A

The Chinese character for "family"

In the 1850s, when Spring Pearl's story takes place, China was a country bound by tradition. For thousands of years, Chinese people lived much as their ancestors had. Children grew up knowing that their family and their culture had been around for a long, long time. One family's record book went back 48 generations—almost a thousand years of history, handed down by parents to their children.

Strict traditions guided the way Chinese people dressed. Married women wore an *aoqin* (ow-chin)—

This elaborately embroidered tunic was worn over a skirt or trousers.

a tunic and a long skirt. Unmarried girls wore an *aoku* (ow-kue)—a tunic and wide trousers. A formal aoku was usually made of silk embroidered with symbols of good fortune and long life, like cranes and plum blossoms. Spring Pearl's mother embroidered camellia flowers on her aoku as a symbol of spring and a play on Spring Pearl's name.

Since Chinese clothes had no pockets, men carried money and papers tucked into their sleeves and trouser cuffs. Girls and women often carried small embroidered drawstring purses.

For good luck, women wore jewelry, such as bracelets and hair ornaments, made of jade. Upper-class women and girls, like Master Sung's daughters, wore elaborate hairstyles. Sometimes a girl slept with her head resting on a block of wood instead of a pillow to keep her hair from coming undone!

Some wealthy girls had tiny bound feet. From the age of three or four, a girl's feet were tightly wrapped, with the toes folded underneath the sole. Over time, this folded shape became permanent, and girls

This drawstring purse with jade beads could be carried or worn around the neck.

This little boy's feet were already larger than his older sisters' bound feet.

hobbled painfully on feet only a few inches long. The Han, the largest ethnic group in China, thought bound feet were beautiful. Foot-binding also showed a family's wealth—females with bound feet needed servants to wait on them. Poor families did not bind their daughters' feet. Neither did Chinese families from other ethnic groups, like the Hakka and the Manchus.

The behavior of Chinese girls was tightly bound by society's expectations, too. Wealthy girls and women rarely went outside the walls of their estates. Girls learned skills such as sewing and embroidery, but most did not learn to read. Boys, in contrast, went to school and were valued more than girls throughout all of Chinese society.

Because famine and hunger could and did come at any time, the Chinese developed a taste for an incredible variety of foods. People in Canton were famously adventurous eaters. Special foods are still a big part of Chinese celebrations, like the moon cakes Auntie Wong made for the Moon Festival and special rice-flour pastries made for the weeklong Chinese New Year celebration.

Canton, the city where Spring Pearl lived, is located on China's south coast and was its biggest port. By the 1850s, this ancient city was a maze of alleys and streets jammed with shops, houses, and temples. Poor families lived in crowded neighborhoods like the Rats' Nest, but wealthy families like the Sungs lived in *compounds*, gracious clusters of houses, buildings, and gardens enclosed by walls.

Even today, Chinese markets offer a wide variety of foods, such as these dried mushrooms and roots.

Cantonese who lived in houseboats or along the shore had more chances to see Europeans.

To preserve its traditional way of life, China's rulers limited contact between foreigners and the Chinese people. For centuries, Europeans were not allowed to mingle with Chinese citizens. China sold vast amounts of silk and tea to the Europeans but bought few goods in return. In the 1840s, Great Britain went to war to force China to open up trade and allow the British to sell *opium*, an addictive drug, in China. The British won the "Opium War," but they were not satisfied.

In 1857, the British and the French again attacked Canton, starting the Second Opium War. The Opium Wars were a turning point in Chinese history, because they opened China to foreign influences.

In the 1850s, many Chinese men were leaving China to make money in the Land of the Golden Mountain—the United States—where the California

Gold Rush was in full swing. Those who came back to China brought new ways with them.

Slowly, China's ancient traditions began to change. Today, girls in China have many more choices than they did in Spring Pearl's time. Foot-binding was outlawed in 1911, and modern Chinese girls go to school, play sports, and use computers.

Girls in China still face prejudice, however. China is overpopulated, so families are allowed to have only one child—and most hope for a boy. Some families abandon infant daughters to try again for a boy. Many abandoned babies are adopted by families from other countries. Though these girls grow up far from their birthplace, many can visit Chinatowns in cities where Chinese immigrants have settled and brought China's traditions to new places.

Chinese society is more open today than in Spring Pearl's time. Girls are educated along with boys and learn about the rest of the world.

Author's Note

If I were to draw a picture of the history of southern China in the 1850s, it would be a row of doorways. In that decade doors began opening for average people. In the story, I mention some of the economic opportunities in China, but many Chinese, including my own family, were also emigrating to America as well as to other countries. To this day, most Chinese Americans can trace their roots back to southern China around Canton.

So, although Spring Pearl lived in the 1850s, I feel as if I've known her all my life. In her independence, her intelligence, and her optimism, she is the ancestor of my Chinatown "aunties." They were not blood relations but rather friends of my mother and my aunts. As Chinese American girls growing up in the 1930s, they did not let the many restrictions and hardships of the times stop them. Among other things they did when they were young, they learned how to fence. They met challenges similar to Spring Pearl's with the same energy and good humor. And like Blessing, I learned the hard way not to play cards or *mah jong* with them for money.

Likewise, I grew up with Doggy, Auntie Wong, Uncle Soo, Hammer, and the other Rats, as well as the Sungs—some of whose descendants I must have bumped into in San Francisco's Chinatown.

The siege of Canton and the description of its streets grow indirectly out of thirty years of research. Like a pack rat, I have acquired books and articles about the life of Chinese Americans both here and in their ancestral area of southern China. From my bookshelves and filing cabinets come the different facts—such as the Canton shops or how to make cloth shoes—that serve as the soil awaiting a character like Spring Pearl to plant a seed that can become a story like *The Last Flower*.

Laurence Yep